'Ivy, what's going on?'

She'd been staring unseeing down at her fingers, which she'd been wrapping and unwrapping around the stem of her champagne glass.

She took a breath. The deepest breath she could remember taking.

Then she lifted her gaze and met his.

Even in the moody bar lighting she now finally had enough light to see the colour of his eyes. Hazel. They were lovely eyes, sexy eyes, but right now they were hard and unyielding.

Yes, he'd worked out that this night wasn't going to pan out the way he'd planned.

'Angus—I'm pregnant.'

Dear Reader

I started writing Ivy and Angus's story just after my daughter turned one. The most amazing—and exhausting!—year of my life had come to an end, and I was finally writing again.

It's probably no surprise that a baby popped into this story! But Ivy's story is very different from mine. Ivy certainly hasn't planned her pregnancy. In fact Ivy falls pregnant at exactly the worst possible moment in her career. For Ivy, her career *is* everything—so it's as if her whole world has collapsed around her. Plus she also has to deal with a gorgeous, charming soldier who just *won't* go away!

I now know first-hand how life-changing children are—in a way I never comprehended before. But what would it be like to share such a life-changing experience with a practical stranger? That question is where Ivy and Angus's story begins, and I just had to keep writing until this unlikely couple made it to their happy-ever-after.

I hope you enjoy Ivy and Angus's story!

Leah

PS I'll let you in on a secret—I often name my heroines using baby names I love but that my husband vetoed. I *still* think Ivy is a beautiful name!

NINE MONTH COUNTDOWN

BY
LEAH ASHTON

ISBN: 978-0-263-24348-2

Harlequin (UK) Limited's policy is to use papers that are natural,
renewable and recyclable products and made from wood grown in
sustainable forests. The logging and manufacturing processes conform
to the legal environmental regulations of the country of origin.

Printed and bound in Great Britain
by CPI Antony Rowe, Chippenham, Wiltshire

An unashamed fan of all things happily-ever-after, **Leah Ashton** has been a lifelong reader of romance. Writing came a little bit later—although in hindsight she's been dreaming up stories for as long as she can remember. Sadly, the most popular boy in school never did suddenly fall head over heels in love with her…

Now she lives in Perth, Western Australia, with her own real-life hero, two gorgeous dogs and the world's smartest cat. By day she works in IT-land; by night she considers herself incredibly lucky to be writing the type of books she loves to read and to have the opportunity to share her own characters' happily-ever-afters with readers.

You can visit Leah at www.leah-ashton.com

Other Modern Tempted™ titles by Leah Ashton:

BEWARE OF THE BOSS
WHY RESIST A REBEL?

This and other titles by Lee Ashton are available in eBook format from www.millsandboon.co.uk

For Regan—
who thinks all my heroes are based on him, but they're not.

You're *my* hero, though, baby.

I'm having so much fun
sharing my happy-ever-after with you.

CHAPTER ONE

IT HAD STARTED exactly eleven steps down the aisle.

Ivy knew this, because she'd been counting.

Step, together *one*. Step, together *two*.

Generally the counting happened when she could feel the famous Molyneux temper bubbling away inside her. Or on the rare occasions she was nervous—although she couldn't remember the last time that had been. But today, it was neither of those things. The bride—her sister April—was the one who should be feeling anxious. Marriage wasn't something Ivy could see herself doing any time soon. She dated, occasionally, but never anything serious. Right now, her focus was on her work, and the family business, and everything else took a back seat. Because in Ivy's experience relationships had an irritating habit of leaching into everything. And when it came to her career, well—anything that could damage *that* was just not acceptable.

But anyway... She'd been walking down the aisle, happily aware that the crowd seated in rows of white wooden chairs were peering around her for a glimpse of the bride, when she'd *felt* it. At exactly step eleven.

Someone wasn't looking around her. Not at all. Someone was looking right at her, in a way that Ivy wouldn't have thought possible. In a way that had *weight*.

And it was so strange, and so unexpected, that Ivy even stopped counting.

But she didn't stop walking, and she didn't shift her gaze from exactly where she was heading: the celebrant, a pretty wooden trellis temporarily constructed on the exclusive Nusa Dua beach, and the cerulean blue of the Indian Ocean beyond. Because today she was April's chief bridesmaid, and she took any job that she was given seriously. Bridesmaid or Board Executive—it didn't matter. Work was work, and Ivy *always* lived by the idea that you should never do *anything* if you weren't going to do it right.

So she started counting afresh, and then made sure she completed her bridesmaid duties to the best of her ability.

But that weight didn't lift until well after April had kissed her new husband. In fact, it wasn't until April and Evan stood together to accept the hugs and well wishes of their guests that Ivy could *finally* openly search the crowd without fear of raising the ire of the videographer.

But by then it was too late. That heavy, heavy gaze was gone.

Much later—what seemed like *hours* of smiling for the photographer later—Ivy stood with her two sisters and the rest of the bridal party at the back of the enormous marquee that would host the wedding reception.

The luxury hotel their mother had booked for the occasion loomed four storeys high on three sides, hugging the marquee as it stared out to the ocean. A welcome whisper of a breeze skimmed Ivy's bare shoulders and pushed the silk of her full-length dress against her legs. It was still warm, but Bali's famous humidity appeared to have let up just a little. Regardless, a blonde make-up artist hovered amongst them, busily 'fixing' Ivy and her sisters before their big entrance. *Can't have your faces melting!*

Ivy shifted her weight rather than rolling her eyes—which reminded her once again that crazily expensive, handmade, bespoke heels did not guarantee comfort. Not even close.

The Balinese wedding planner was barking out instructions in a failed attempt at a stage whisper, but having reviewed the day's minute schedule—and provided a few useful suggestions—Ivy knew exactly where she should be. She strode over to Sean, Evan's best mate—and best man—and hooked her arm through his.

'Are we going in?' he asked. Beer in hand, he clearly wasn't taking his best-man duties as seriously as Ivy would've liked.

In fact, the music April had chosen for their entrance had started, so Ivy used her free hand to pluck the beer from Sean, and to hand it to the wedding planner.

'And we just follow them?' Sean asked as he watched Mila and Ed disappear into the marquee.

'You *were* at the rehearsal, right?' Ivy said, but she was smiling as she tugged Sean behind her.

Inside, the marquee opened up—it was only the rear wall that had, well, *a wall*. Otherwise it was edged with white fabric gathered curtain-like against each support. April's two-hundred-odd guests sat at white-draped tables topped with ivory flower arrangements amongst dozens of sparkling chandeliers—and beyond them, framed by the marquee like a postcard, was the ocean. Of course, a Molyneux wedding would never be anything less than spectacular—but even Ivy was impressed. And timing their entrance *just* as the sun began to sink beneath the darkening blue of the ocean? Perfect.

Ivy was about halfway to the bridal table when she realised she was counting her steps again.

Thirty-two. Thirty-three. Thirty-four...

But this time it annoyed her. Maybe it was the distraction of...of whatever it was she thought she'd felt during the ceremony—or maybe it was just that it kind of made sense that she'd be a bit tense while walking down the aisle, given her feelings about love and relationships. So counting her steps then had been okay.

But now? No, it wasn't acceptable. Because now she recognised why she was doing it.

She *was* nervous. The way her stomach was flip-flopping all over the place made that crystal-clear.

Why?

She was used to having so many eyes on her. How many times had she been the spokesperson for Molyneux Mining? She had years of media training behind her. She'd been interviewed on live television, and she'd been splashed all over the newspapers—accurately and otherwise—her entire life.

So, yes, nineteen-year-old Ivy counted her steps *all* the time. Twenty-seven-year-old Ivy a hell of a lot less. Now, *thirty-one*-year-old Chief Operating Officer of Molyneux Mining Ivy shouldn't need to do it at all.

Thirty-one-year-old Ivy was an accomplished, confident—*powerful*, some might say—*grown-up*. Counting steps was just…juvenile.

Fifty-seven. Fifty-eight. Fifty—

'What did I do?' Sean asked as he pulled out her spindly chair at the long bridal table.

Ivy blinked. 'Pardon?'

'You just told me to "Stop it".' He looked at her curiously. 'With some force.'

'I didn't,' she said, very quickly. Then sat down and fussed needlessly with her silverware as Sean took his own seat.

Ignoring Sean's gaze, Ivy looked up to watch April glide across the marquee, arm in arm with her new husband—and both with stars in their eyes.

Her little sister had never looked more beautiful: like a princess with her blonde hair piled up high, and the oversized skirt of her dress floating about her like a cloud.

Ivy couldn't help but smile, the ridiculous mystery of the

step counting put aside for the moment. She was so happy for April. Today was her dream come true.

Slowly she relaxed into her chair, allowing that inexplicable tension to ease from her body.

And it was right about then—right about when she decided that *yes*, it was totally fine to slide her heels off beneath the privacy of the long table cloth—that she felt it again.

That look. *That* heavy concentration of attention that made the back of her neck prickle, but other parts of her... tingle. And Ivy was not one for superfluous *tingling*.

But this time there was nothing stopping her from looking up—from searching the crowd for this person, for this...

Man.

There he was, on the opposite side of the parquet dance floor. With his close-cropped hair, and the broadest of broad shoulders, Ivy would've guessed he was in the military, even if she hadn't already known he was.

Angus. His name was Angus...Something. She remembered his name had stood out amongst April's seating plan and guest list—a name she didn't recognise, and who April also didn't know. An old school friend of Evan's: *All I know is that he's a soldier,* April had whispered with some awe, *one of those special ones. SAS.*

Amongst a million other wedding-planning things to do—and a million more work-related concerns—she hadn't given the mysterious Angus Somebody another thought.

But right now, the man had somehow taken up *all* her thoughts. And when their gazes finally connected—when she could truly *see* all that remarkable intensity—it was almost as if he'd taken over her body, too. Her skin was hot. Her mouth was dry.

And from this distance, she couldn't even see the colour of his eyes.

Oh, God. What would happen if he was close enough for her to see if they were blue, or green, or grey?

Based on her current reaction, she'd most likely burst into flames.

No.

Now she was being silly. He was just a man, just a guest at the wedding.

Just a distraction she didn't need.

She was April's chief bridesmaid. And she was Chief Operating Officer of Molyneux Mining. Neither of those things were conducive to gazing like a lust-crazed idiot across the dance floor at her sister's wedding.

Yet she was still doing exactly that.

And just as she was sternly telling herself that it really wasn't that hard to look elsewhere…*anywhere*…but at *him*…

Something happened.

He winked.

Angus Barlow always knew what he was doing. He was measured, methodical, structured. Calm. Not easily distracted, or swayed by others.

So he'd known what he'd been doing when his gaze had first collided with Ivy as she'd walked down that aisle. He'd been having a damn good look at a beautiful woman.

Her long black hair was looped and twisted up to leave her neck exposed above her bare shoulders. Her skin had glowed in the sunlight, and was still managing to do so now, even in the candlelit marquee without the help of the rapidly setting sun.

She had a great profile. A long, thin nose and a strong chin.

The sea breeze had done fabulous things to the pale purple dress she wore, plastering it hard against her curves as she'd walked. And if he'd continued to watch her rear view, rather than turning to observe the bride's arrival—well, Angus didn't really think anyone could blame him.

And now, hours later, he'd found himself again compelled to look at Ivy.

Angus supposed it could be argued that Ivy wasn't the most beautiful woman at the wedding. In fact, Angus had heard that many considered her unlucky she didn't inherit more of her father's movie-star looks, the way her two younger sisters had. Although Angus couldn't agree. It was true she did take more after her unusual mother—in both looks and personality, given the way she was following exactly in her mother's business footsteps. But he liked the angles to Ivy's face: the sharpness of her cheekbones, the slant to her brows.

Plus he'd *really* liked the contrasting plump of her lips. He'd never noticed before tonight, never really even looked at the many photos of her that could be found in the paper, or the footage of her on TV. But right now it seemed impossible he hadn't.

So yes, he did know what he was doing.

Right on cue, he felt a twinge in his bandaged right wrist, as if to remind him at least partly *why* he was doing this.

Not why he was looking at Ivy Molyneux. But why he was here, at this wedding, at all.

He wasn't supposed to be here, of course. He'd declined the original invitation, only to break his wrist during a training exercise in Darwin a month or so later.

So rather than where he *should* be, deployed with his squadron in Afghanistan, he was at Evan's wedding. Surrounded by people who were part of a world he'd exited so abruptly more than fifteen years earlier, and that he'd truly not missed at all.

This was not his thing: an opulent, diamond-drenched evening jammed full of the superficial and the vacuous.

He was on a singles table of sorts. His fellow guests

were a mixture of the different flavours of wealth he remembered from high school: old money, new money, and used-to-have money. Then there were the people aware of their luck and good fortune—and then those that were painfully, frustratingly oblivious. In his experience, most of the wealthy fell into the second category. But even then, they generally weren't bad people. Just not his type of people.

Ivy Molyneux was certainly not his type of people either. A billionaire heiress born into obscene wealth, how could she be anything but extraordinarily ignorant of what it was like to actually exist in the real world?

And yet that was the thing. Amongst the hundreds of faces here at this wedding, amongst all this glitz and glitter, when she'd met his gaze it had felt...

Real.

That he certainly hadn't expected.

That was why he hadn't looked away, and why his interest in her had become *much* more than a simple visual appreciation of a beautiful woman.

That was why he'd winked.

And Ivy's jaw had dropped open, then almost immediately snapped shut.

Then her eyes had narrowed, just before a near imperceptible shake of her head—and she'd turned her attention to the groomsman beside her, as if Angus no longer existed.

But somehow he knew, knew deep within his bones, that this wasn't even close to over.

It had taken considerable effort, but Ivy managed to avoid looking at Angus throughout her entire maid of honour speech. Thanks to years of practising public speaking, Ivy knew how to ensure the entire crowd felt she was talking directly to them. Unfortunately tonight the block of about five tables immediately surrounding Angus's might have felt rather ignored.

But, it couldn't be helped.

Not that the not looking helped a lot. Because he'd definitely just kept on looking at her.

She knew it, because her whole body felt his concentrated attention. It had only been sheer will that had prevented the stupid racing of her heart or the odd, inexplicable nerves that churned through her belly from impacting her voice. Honestly, she felt as though, if she let herself, she'd come over all soft and breathy and...*pathetic*.

But of course she hadn't, and April had given her the tightest of hugs after her speech, so that was a relief. That was all that mattered tonight, that April was happy.

Even her mother—on the parents' table in prime position near the cake—had lifted her chin in the subtlest of actions. Ivy had learnt long ago that that was about as effusive as Irene Molyneux ever got, so she'd take it.

With her formal duties out of the way, Ivy should now be able to relax for the remainder of the speeches. But of course she couldn't.

By the time dessert was served, and Evan had delivered his—hilarious by the reaction of the guests, even if Ivy registered barely a word—speech, Ivy was about to crawl out of her skin in frustration.

Finally the dancing began—and Ivy made her escape.

With the straps of her heels tangled in her fingers, the lawn outside the marquee was cool beneath her bare feet. She had to walk some distance before she could hear the ocean above the exuberant cacophony of music and voices of the reception.

The hotel gardens stretched along the beach from either side of the main hotel building. Lights dotted pathways that led to bungalows and villas, but they were all empty, with every guest at the hotel also a guest at the wedding.

And it felt empty, which Ivy appreciated. She'd flown in from London only...yesterday? No, the day before.

Ivy smiled—it was recently enough, anyway, that jet lag still had her confusing her days.

But after a series of intense business meetings, a thirty-six-hour journey from London after delays in Dubai, the madness that was the last-minute planning for the wedding, and then that disconcerting attention from Angus Whoever—Ivy was seriously happy to finally be *alone*.

She took a long, measured breath and waited for her muscles to relax as she exhaled.

But they didn't.

'Ivy.'

She spun around to confront the reason for the tension throughout her body. Angus wore a cream linen shirt, untucked, and dark knee-length tailored shorts—a variation of what the majority of male guests were wearing. Unlike the majority of male guests, he still managed what should be impossible—to look as if he was attending a wedding, rather than a barbeque. Maybe it was his posture? The extreme straightness of how he stood, combined with the way his clothing hung so perfectly from his muscular frame? Whatever it was, Ivy suspected he looked equally gorgeous taking out his garbage.

'You followed me,' she said.

He shrugged. 'You knew I would.'

Ivy's mouth dropped open. 'Don't be absurd.'

While his shirt was clearly visible in the limited light, the rest of him blurred into the darkness behind him, his face all angles and shadows. Even so, Ivy knew, *knew*, he was looking at her in disbelief.

'Look,' she said, in her no-nonsense work voice, 'I really don't have time for this.'

'This being?'

He really did have a fantastic voice. Deep and authoritative.

Not that it made any difference.

'*This,*' she said, waving her hands to encompass them both.

'I'm still confused,' he said. 'Can you elaborate?'

Ivy gave a little huff of frustration. 'I don't have time for whatever two random strangers might do when they meet at a wedding.'

And she didn't. It had been hours since she'd checked her email.

A laugh. 'C'mon, Ivy. I'm sure you can think up a far more interesting descriptor than *whatever.*'

'I could,' she said. 'But that would take more of my precious time. So—'

She was half a step towards the path when Angus's hand wrapped around her lower arm. He wore a light bandage that encircled his palm and extended halfway to his elbow, the fabric just the tiniest bit rough against her skin.

'Honey, *everyone* has time for...' his grip loosened and his fingers briefly traced a path across her wrist '...talking.'

Ignoring her body's traitorous shivery reaction to his touch, Ivy went on the defensive. 'This isn't just talking.'

But, of course, that was a mistake.

She sensed, rather than saw, his smile.

'No,' he said. 'That's the point, isn't it?'

Ivy shook her head, as if that would somehow help her brain reorganise itself. She was just...off. Unbalanced. If she was to walk away from him now, she'd be counting her steps, definitely.

'No,' she said. 'The point is there *is* no point. That's the point.' Seriously? Could she be any more ridiculous?

She tried again. 'You're not my type, Angus.'

The shadow of his smile told her immediately that she'd made a mistake. Now he knew she knew his name.

But standing so close to him, Ivy supposed she should be relieved she could speak at all. What did this man do to her?

'I don't believe you,' he said. As if that was that.

And then he surprised her by casually sitting on the sand. He leant right back on his elbows, his legs crossed at the ankles. 'Sit.'

Logic would've had her back at the marquee by now, so it came as no surprise that she found herself seated beside him. She sat more stiffly though, her hands rested on the silk skirt that covered her knees, her gaze firmly on the black of the ocean.

A big part of her knew she really needed to get back to the marquee. What if April needed her? Plus it really had been hours since she'd checked her email—maybe she could pop by her suite on the way back?

She'd levered herself onto her knees to stand when she felt Angus's hand on her arm. Electricity shot across her skin and she found herself completely still.

'Hey,' he said. 'We're supposed to be having a conversation, remember?'

'But, my emails—'

The man's laughter was loud, and strong and totally unexpected in the darkness.

'Emails? You're on a deserted tropical beach with a guy who is seriously attracted to you—and you're thinking about email? That cuts deep.'

Ivy smiled despite herself, and rearranged her legs so she was sitting again, his hand—unfortunately—falling away.

'You're seriously attracted to me?' she said.

'I'll take smug if it means no more talk of work.'

Ivy smiled again. 'Deal,' she said. For a long minute, she studied the ocean again. Her eyes had adjusted now, and she could just make out the occasional edge of foam along the crest of a wave.

Something had changed, Ivy realised. The stiffness in her shoulders had loosened. A tightness in her jaw was gone.

She couldn't say she was relaxed, not sitting beside this

man. But the tension she felt had shifted—maybe it was that her everyday tensions had lifted? Only to be replaced by another flavour of tension, but Ivy had to admit the tension that radiated between her and Angus was vastly, vastly preferable—no matter how uncomfortable it felt.

Uncomfortable, because she didn't know what to do with it. But also…different. Unfamiliar. Exciting.

She twisted to face him.

'Hi, I'm Ivy Molyneux,' she said.

'Angus Barlow.'

And she smiled. It had been an intense few days, so frantic that she'd barely acknowledged her beautiful surroundings.

For the first time, she really felt the beach sand beneath her toes. Felt the kiss of the ocean breeze.

She deserved a break, even if she didn't have time for a holiday.

And really, what was the harm of letting her guard down with a gorgeous, charming stranger, just for a few minutes?

Then she'd go check her email, and then back to the wedding.

Simple.

CHAPTER TWO

VERY CALMLY, IVY snapped the clear lid over the end of the test, and took a long, deep soothing breath.

She was sitting on the closed lid of a toilet. A very nice toilet in a very expensive Perth skyscraper, but a toilet, none the less. A public toilet.

This had been a very stupid idea.

Buying the test itself had seemed the rational thing to do this morning. Her driver, Simon, hadn't suspected a thing when she'd asked him to stop at a pharmacy on the way to her ten a.m. meeting. And even if he had wondered why Ivy Molyneux was bothering to run into a pharmacy for whatever lady thing he thought she needed—rather than asking one of her assistants—it wasn't as if he'd ask her.

Yet she'd still fidgeted in the back seat of the car as they'd driven away, as if Simon had X-ray vision and could see through the layers of her handbag and pharmacy paper bag should he glance in his rear-view mirror.

The plan had been to wait until she was home this evening. Safely alone in the privacy of her home in Peppermint Grove, where she could pee on a stick and irrationally stress and worry *alone* for the two minutes she was supposed to wait because—come on, it was *totally normal* to be two days late, even if that had never, ever, ever happened before...

Of *course* someone else had just walked into the bathroom, and now she had to wait in this excruciating state as she listened to the other woman pee—because it now seemed beyond her to look down, to look down at the test that by now would display the result.

The reality.

All she had to do was look down and this would all be over.

This *thing*, this *day*, this *moment* that she had not expected at all. *That* night seemed a lifetime ago. April was already back from her honeymoon. Ivy's work days had been as endless as ever and her weekends had been so blurred into her weeks that she'd barely noticed them. Life had gone on. She'd gone on, just as normal. That night— that *totally out of character* night—was long behind her. She hadn't given it, or Angus, another thought.

Well, barely. Maybe, just maybe, when she'd been in that space between wake and sleep when her brain finally emptied of all things Molyneux Mining, *maybe* she'd let herself remember. Remember the way her skin had shivered when Angus had looked at her. The way her heart had zipped to a million beats a minute when he'd finally touched her. How she'd felt in his arms. How *he'd* felt beneath her fingertips.

How it had *all* felt. To do that. To do something so crazy, so uninhibited, so…

Reckless.

The toilet flushed beside her, then footsteps, and then the cubicle door closed. The basin had some silly sensor arrangement to turn on, and Ivy had to wait as the other woman tried to work it out, and then listen to her jump and giggle when the water finally gushed out.

Just go. Just go, just go, just go.

But also just stay. Stay, stay, stay for ever, so she never had to look down, never had to know.

But then she wasn't into delaying things, was she? That was why she was here, in this public toilet, holding the test.

Because she couldn't wait. Couldn't even wait until her

ten a.m. meeting was over. She'd excused herself mid meeting, and now she'd taken way, way too long.

The bathroom door clicked shut, and Ivy was finally alone amongst all this marble and the softest of background music.

And now she had to look down.

And now she couldn't lie to herself that she was just being silly, and that there was *nothing* to worry about, and that she was on the pill and even if she couldn't be sure she hadn't forgotten a pill amongst all the time zones and delays on the way to April's wedding that surely the odds were *still* in her favour. Because people tried to do this for *years* and it didn't work. People who were trying, people who wanted this, people…

Two pink lines.

She'd looked down only to confirm what she already knew. What she'd known deep down for the past two-hundred-odd minutes since the absence of her period had suddenly dawned on her.

She was pregnant.

She was pregnant.

Ivy took a deep, audible breath, and willed the tears in her eyes to go still. Then she stuffed the test back into its box, back into its pharmacy paper bag and back into her handbag.

Then she went back to the meeting with her business face on and no one—she hoped liked hell—was the wiser.

No, only one person knew that Ivy Molyneux's life had just completely fallen apart.

And unfortunately, that number would soon have to increase to two.

Angus's feet pounded on the heavy rubber of the treadmill, his breaths coming slow and regular.

Sweat had long ago soaked his grey T-shirt black, and

the muscles of his calves and thighs had given up protesting and now simply burned.

This was the bit he loved. This time after he'd conquered the arguments from both his brain and body and simply *kept on going.*

He'd been like this since his late teens, since the sudden death of his father. He'd gone for his first run immediately after his mum had told him the terrible news—an impossibly long run fuelled by intense, raging grief. And that run had triggered a near addiction that had him craving the adrenalin rush of exercise, craving the burn, and craving the pain.

He had no issue admitting that one of the reasons he'd joined the army was so he could be paid to reach this high. On some days he couldn't believe his luck that he earned his living effectively living out many a childhood fantasy—the helicopters, the firearms, the boats, the tactical training...

Angus shook his head as he ran, shifting his focus back to his body.

Running on a treadmill was not his preference. Here in the gym at the barracks, he'd much rather be lifting weights, or, even better, completing a punishing PT session with the rest of his squadron.

But when it came down to it, the method was irrelevant. Winning the battle over his body was what mattered. Especially now, especially while injured.

Technically he was on medical leave, but clearly losing physical condition wasn't an option in his job. He'd been down at the barracks daily, excluding that weekend in Bali. Even there he'd made locating the hotel gym a priority.

Except the morning after the wedding. That morning he'd slept in.

Despite the sweat and the screaming of his muscles, Angus grinned.

Ivy must have worn him out.

He reached out to slow the speed on the treadmill, reducing his pace from near sprint down to a brisk walk as he cooled down.

It wasn't the first time the beautiful billionaire had popped into his head. It surprised him. There had been no question as to what that night had been. Neither he nor Ivy wanted anything beyond those few…admittedly incredible…hours on that beach.

Angus smiled again as he remembered the way Ivy had taken charge as they'd walked back to the hotel.

If anyone asks—I was in my suite, working.

He'd grinned then, too. *And how would I know that?*

She'd just glared at him, and protested silently when he insisted on walking her to her room. He had, of course, checked that no one would see them.

He wasn't a total jerk, after all.

Although kissing her on her doorstep had not been gentlemanly—or planned.

He'd seen it in her eyes—and felt it in her body—that she'd been about to invite him in. But she hadn't.

And he would've declined, anyway. He was sure.

It was for the best.

In his experience, keeping things simple was always for the best.

Later, after his shower and as he walked across the car park, he felt his phone vibrating in the backpack slung over his shoulder. Automatically he fished it out, then, on seeing it was an unknown number, considered for a moment whether he should bother answering.

Work-related numbers weren't stored on his phone, of course—but then, no one was going to be calling him while he was on leave.

But could it be to do with his mum?

So he answered it, if a bit gruffly, and was certainly not

expecting the contradictory soft but firm—and *familiar*—female voice he heard.

'Is that Angus Barlow?'

'Ivy Molyneux,' he replied, and then smiled when she gave a little sound of surprise.

'Uh—yes,' she said. A pause. 'I asked Evan for your number.'

She was nervous, her words brisker than normal.

'That wasn't very discreet,' he said.

Hell, it didn't bother him. Ivy could've announced the fact they'd had sex on the beach to the whole wedding reception and he wouldn't have cared.

But he knew she did.

Unease prickled at the back of his neck.

'No, it wasn't discreet at all,' Ivy said, her words pancake flat.

Then there was a long, long pause.

'Why did you call me, Ivy?' He *was* gruff now.

She cleared her throat. 'Are you free tonight?' she asked, much more softly.

Relief washed over him. He'd continued walking as they'd been talking, and now he propped a shoulder against the side of his black SUV.

He smiled. He remembered that tone from that night. That soft, intimate—almost *shy*—voice. So different from the brash confidence of Ivy Molyneux, mining executive.

He was jumping at shadows. Ivy Molyneux was a woman who went after what she wanted. This phone call was nothing more. Unexpected, but also—not unwelcome.

'I'm free,' he said. 'How about we meet at Ms Black at eight?'

A wine bar in Subiaco he'd visited with the rest of his squadron after they'd returned from their latest assignment—before they'd quickly relocated to the pub next door. It was sophisticated, intimate, stunning. Very Ivy.

'Fine,' she said. 'I—uh—guess I'll see you there.'

'Ivy—' he said, before she had the chance to hang up. 'I'm still not after anything serious.'

He felt it was important he was honest.

But judging by her almost shriek of laughter before she ended the call, he had nothing to worry about on that front, regardless.

How had she let this happen?

For what felt like the hundredth time, Ivy had to stop herself fidgeting. So far she'd swivelled her bar stool, kicked her heels against the foot rest and attempted to tear a coaster into a million pieces.

She'd counted every step she'd made tonight. From her house to her car, and then from where her driver dropped her right outside this incredibly trendy bar to this seat. It was *ridiculous*.

In front of her sat an untouched glass of champagne.

She didn't even know why she'd ordered it. Out of habit? Or denial?

Ha!

As if it weren't the only thought reverberating about her head.

I'm pregnant. I'm pregnant. I'm pregnant.

How had she let this happen?

This being pregnant. *This* being dressed in a cute cocktail dress on a Thursday night to tell a man *she didn't even know* something that would change his life for ever.

The dress was new. She'd dragged one of her assistants out shopping. Ivy had made sure she'd smiled a lot and dropped hints about her 'date' tonight while still being deliberately coy.

That was all that had kept her going as the seconds and minutes had crawled along—focusing on her...*plan*.

In all honesty, it was far from her best plan. In fact, it was most likely her worst.

But she needed a plan right now. She needed a way forward, a way to fix this.

Because Ivy Molyneux didn't make mistakes.

'Ivy.'

At the sound of Angus's already familiar deep voice, Ivy channelled Julia Roberts in *Pretty Woman* as she slowly pivoted her chair to face him. What she really wanted to do was disappear between the floorboards. So, so badly.

But then she saw him.

In Bali, in his casual wedding attire, he'd been undeniably handsome. Heck, he'd be undeniably handsome *anywhere.*

But in the intimate lighting of the bar, in dark jeans, boots and a slim fitting black shirt he was…just plain gorgeous. His clothes weren't particularly formal, but he somehow managed to still look effortlessly dressed to impress. He looked darker, taller, *broader* than she remembered.

Especially now that he was standing so close to her. Close enough to touch.

And then he did touch her. Casually leaning forward to brush a kiss against her cheek and to bring his lips to her ear.

'You are stunning,' he said. His breath momentarily tickled her neck.

Ivy shivered.

He stepped back, his appreciative gaze sweeping over her.

She loved the dress she'd bought today. Teal silk with a feminine wrap bodice and a fitted skirt that hit mid-thigh, it flattered her curves and on any other day would've made her feel on top of the world.

That it didn't helped bring her back to reality.

This wasn't a date.

This *so* wasn't a date.

Ivy slid off her chair, waving away the arm he offered her. Without a word she headed to the back of the bar. It was busy, with all but the three tables along the far wall occupied.

Each was marked with a small reserved sign, and it was towards the middle table that Ivy gestured.

'I booked a table,' she said.

She'd booked three, actually, and paid for a night's worth of meals on all. It was still hardly private, but it would have to do.

'Dinner?' Angus asked.

Despite everything, Ivy managed a smile. Clearly dinner and conversation were not what Angus had planned for the night.

He was close beside her, and she could practically feel his growing tension.

Well, that situation wasn't about to improve for him.

She took her seat, and Angus took his. He must have plucked her champagne from the bar, as he placed it before her, his wrist still bandaged as it had been in Bali.

That was nice of him.

Would he be a good dad?

She gave a little shake of her head. No. This wasn't fair, that she knew and he didn't. That he thought he was here for meaningless flirtation followed by meaningless sex, when he so, so wasn't.

'Ivy, what's going on?'

She'd been staring, unseeing, down at her fingers, which she'd been wrapping and unwrapping around the stem of her champagne glass.

She took a breath. The deepest breath she could remember taking.

Then she lifted her gaze, and met his.

Even in the moody bar lighting, she now finally had enough light to see the colour of his eyes. Hazel.

They were lovely eyes, sexy eyes, but right now they were hard and unyielding.

Yes, he'd worked out that this night wasn't going to pan out the way he'd planned.

'Angus—I'm pregnant.'

CHAPTER THREE

PREGNANT?

All the stupid, obvious questions were on the tip of his tongue.

Are you sure?

How…?

Is it mine?

But he knew all the answers:

Of course she was. That she wanted to be anywhere but here was clear in everything about her. She was one hundred per cent sure or she wouldn't be putting either of them through this.

The how hardly needed explaining. He'd been there, too.

And was it his?

Well, that was only a faint hope that this was all a terrible mistake, rather than a genuine question.

And he was grateful that a small smidgen of his brain told him to swallow the words before they leapt from his mouth.

Because of course it was his. He had known what he'd been doing in Bali—known he'd pushed her out of her comfort zone, known he'd pursued the electric attraction between them to what he'd felt was the only logical conclusion…

But that she didn't normally have random sex with a practical stranger on a beach had been abundantly clear.

So yes, it was his.

With the basics covered, he dropped his head, gripping his skull with his hands.

He swore harshly.

That was about the sum of it.

'Angus?'

He kept his head down, but he nodded.

'I know this is a shock. I know this is the wrong place to tell you. When I called I hadn't planned this…but…'

It didn't matter. Who cared where she told him?

His thoughts leapt all over the place, as if his brain was incapable of being still, or of grasping onto anything at all.

He'd never felt like this.

He'd been in combat many more times than once.

He'd been in the most stressful situations that most people could imagine. Real stress. Real life-and-death stress, not running-late-for-work stress.

And yet *this* had thrown him. This had sent his ability to think, and apparently to talk, skittering off the rails.

'Um, the thing is, Angus, I have a plan.'

His gaze shot up, linking with hers in almost desperation. 'A plan?'

Ivy nodded slowly. And then she seemed to realise what he was thinking.

She looked down, studying her untouched champagne glass again.

'No,' she said, so softly he had to lean closer. 'Not that.' Her gaze darted back to his, and she looked at him steadfastly now. With that directness, that *realness* he'd liked so much in Bali. 'I'm thirty-one, and I have money and every resource I could wish for at my disposal. In every possible way this is the *last* thing I want. But a termination isn't an option for me.'

She barely blinked as she studied him. Long, long moments passed.

Angus cleared his throat. 'I'm thirty-four with a career I love that takes me away from home for months at a time and could one day kill me. I don't want this. I don't want

children.' Ivy's gaze wobbled a little now as Angus swallowed. 'But for no reason I can fathom, I'm glad you've
made that decision.'

Now he glanced away. He didn't know why he'd said
that, or why he felt that way. The logical part of him—
which was basically *all* of him—didn't understand it.

It made no sense. But it was the truth. His truth.

When he looked back at Ivy she was again studying her
champagne glass.

'Well, it's good we're on the same page, then,' she said,
her tone now brisk and verging on businesslike. 'So, here's
my *actual* plan.' By the time she met his gaze again, she
was all business. Ivy Molyneux of Molyneux Mining—not
Ivy the girl from the beach. 'I'll get straight to the crux of
it: I'd like us to get married.'

Straight after the pregnancy news, Angus would've
thought it would take a hell of a lot to shock him.

That did it.

'What?'

She held up a hand. 'Just hear me out,' she said. 'What
I'm proposing is a business arrangement.' A pause, and
then a half-smile. 'And, yes, marriage.'

Ivy might find this funny, but Angus sure as hell didn't.

He remained stonily silent.

'The term of the agreement would be twelve months
from today,' Ivy continued, clearly warming to her topic.
'As soon as possible we would reveal our—until now—several months' long secret relationship to family and friends,
and, shortly after, our engagement. Then, of course, our—'
now she stumbled a little '—our, um, *situation* would mean
that we'd bring our wedding forward. I thought that we
could make that work in our favour. A Christmas Eve wedding would be perfect, I felt.'

A Christmas Eve wedding would be perfect?

Angus's brain was still requiring most of its synapses

to deal with his impending parenthood. But what little remained was functioning well enough to realise that this
was *completely and utterly nuts*.

'Is this a pregnancy hormone thing?' he asked, quite seriously. 'Can they send you loopy?'

Ivy's gaze hardened. 'I can assure you I am *not* crazy.'

More than anything, Angus wished he'd had time to
order a drink. For want of another option, he gestured at
Ivy's champagne. It wasn't as if she could have it, after all.

She nodded impatiently, and then carried on with her
outrageous proposal as he downed half the drink in one
gulp.

'After the wedding we'd need to continue the illusion
that we're a couple, but given the nature of your work that
shouldn't be too hard. My house is huge, so we could live
quite separate lives when you are home. Not being seen in
public together will help, anyway, for when we separate a
few months after the baby is born.'

She blinked when she said *baby*, as if she couldn't quite
believe it was true.

'After the separation you're free to do whatever you like,
and then, as soon as legally allowable, we'll divorce, and
carry on with our lives.'

'Except for the fact that we're parents of a child we had
together.'

A reluctant nod. 'Well, yes.'

Angus took a second long swig to finish the champagne
he'd barely tasted. He plonked the glass down with little
care, and then leant forward, watching Ivy's eyes widen.

'Why?' he asked.

Ivy actually shrugged. 'Does it matter? I can assure you
that the remuneration you'll receive for this will be a life-
changing amount. Millions of dollars.'

Pocket change to her.

'And a house, too, if you like,' she added, as if an afterthought.

'Before tonight, Ivy, I never wanted children, and I never wanted to get married,' he said. 'Now I'm having a child, but, I can assure you, absolutely nothing has changed on the marriage front. I wouldn't have picked you to be the old-fashioned sort, Ivy, but I'm not. Even with a diamond-encrusted solid-gold carrot.'

Ivy shook her head, as if she couldn't comprehend his rapid refusal. 'I promise you that this will cause you minimal impact, I—'

'It's *marriage*, Ivy. Nothing minimal impact about that.'

She gave a little huff of frustration. 'Don't think of it like that. Think of it as signing a contract, nothing more.'

'Signing a contract of *marriage*, Ivy. And you still haven't told me why.'

Now that he had her glass, Ivy had transferred her fidgeting to her fingers—tangling and twining them together.

Had she really thought he'd agree, just like that? An offer of a crazy amount of money and all sorted? Even if her proposal made no sense on any level?

He studied her. Was she was so detached and separate from reality in her billionaire's turret that she truly believed that money *could* buy her anything? It was his immediate and rather angry conclusion.

He could feel every sinew in his body tense in frustration at the thought of the level of entitlement, of arrogance that would lead to such an assumption...

But now as he looked at Ivy, it didn't fit. He hadn't seen it in her in Bali, and he still didn't recognise it now.

Sure, she was still some distance from *normal*, but he knew it wasn't entitlement, or arrogance, that had triggered her plan.

It was something he could understand. That he could recognise.

It was desperation.

Ivy didn't know what to do now.

Maybe he was right. Maybe pregnancy hormones *had* sent her loopy, because, honestly—had she really thought he'd just agree?

In her experience some people could be bought for the right price. Actually, make that many, many people. But nothing about Angus had indicated to her that he was one of those people. In fact, if she'd spent even a minute properly considering her plan, she would've seen this fatal flaw.

Which of course was the problem. She hadn't spent any time thinking about it, at least not thinking about such pesky details like: *what if he doesn't agree?* Because she'd been clinging to this plan as if it were a rope suspended over the abyss that was her pregnancy, and she just couldn't, could *not*, let it go.

But, the thing was, if this plan had something to do with mineral exploration or extraction, she certainly wouldn't give up this early in the fight.

And that meant that she'd have to—at least partly—answer his question.

'When I turn thirty-two,' she said, looking him in the eye just as she always did during business negotiations, 'my mother will relinquish her position as Chief Executive Officer of Molyneux Mining to me. It's the same age she was when my grandfather died and left her the company, and this has been planned literally from when I was born.' She paused. 'I turn thirty-two in July next year. Based on some useful internet calculators—pending me seeing a doctor—our baby will arrive approximately one week before that date.'

Our baby. A slip of the tongue, but Angus displayed no reaction.

'Although the succession plan was determined before *my* birth, I can assure you that I want this too. I'm very different from my mother in many ways.' A huge understatement. 'But in this way, we are in sync. We both live for Molyneux Mining. This is incredibly important to me.'

It is everything to me, she almost added. But somehow she didn't think that would help.

It was near impossible to read Angus's expression, but he nodded. 'I get that you love your job. I get that you don't want to give that up. What has this got to do with marrying me?'

'About ten years ago just under half of Molyneux Mining was listed on the Australian Stock Exchange. We're still majority family owned, but I report to a board of executives, as well as to our shareholders. We also have a number of significant projects in progress, including a joint venture to mine manganese in the Pilbara, which is reaching final negotiations. It is also widely known that I will take over Molyneux Mining next year, and that we are already in a period of comprehensive change management.'

'So you're worried that a baby will impact your share price?'

Ivy's eyes narrowed. 'No, not the baby. No one had better think that a baby will impact my professional performance.'

Oh, how she *hoped* that was true. She ignored Angus's mildly incredulous raised eyebrows.

'It's all about how the baby came to be here, that's the problem. My whole career has led to my next birthday. Everything I have done, every decision I have made, has been with this succession in the front of my mind. I am known for being meticulous in my planning. For never making a snap decision, for never being reactive in my actions. Even my boyfriends have been chosen with some consideration for my career—I always do background checks. I never take anything or anyone on face value.'

Except she'd never done a background check on Angus. The only thing she'd cared about that night was how good Angus had made her feel.

'So a baby is okay. But hot, crazy sex on a beach with a stranger isn't.'

Ivy recoiled a little, and felt her cheeks grow warm.

Now her gaze dipped to her fingers. With some effort she untangled them, laying her palms flat on the table to force them still.

'I wouldn't have put it quite like that,' she said. 'But yes. Ivy Molyneux would *never* be that reckless.'

There was that word again. Reckless.

This time it triggered a remembered snatch of conversation, the echo of her mother's voice from a time for ever ago: *How could you, Ivy? How could you be so reckless?*

'But you were,' Angus said. 'We both were. I was there.'

His low words snapped Ivy's attention back from a better-forgotten memory. And something flickered in his eyes. Despite all this, despite this situation, despite this conversation, she recognised it.

Heat. Not like in Bali, but still there. Despite everything.

She knew her already warm cheeks were now scarlet, but all she could do was ignore that. And, as she should've at the wedding, ignore this *thing* between them.

Or at least try to.

'I know,' she said, very softly. 'That's what I'm trying to fix.'

The shocking warmth of his hand covering hers drew her attention downwards again, and she realised belatedly she must've been wringing her hands.

She'd trained herself out of all her fidgeting and step counting years ago, but right now this unexpected regres-

sion managed barely a blip amongst everything else that
whirled inside her.

As in Bali, his touch impacted everything. She knew
her heart had accelerated, and her whole body now seemed
focused on where their fingers overlapped. Completely inappropriate warmth pooled low in her belly, and for long
seconds Ivy wished like anything that this were a very
real date.

But then Angus spoke.

'I get what you're trying to do, Ivy,' he said.

Instantly hope began to blossom inside her, delicate and
beautiful. But then his fingers tightened gently on hers,
and Ivy knew.

'My answer is still no.'

And for the second time today awful, unwelcome tears
filled her vision.

Ivy never cried.

But then, Ivy never did a lot of things she'd been doing
lately.

She snatched her hands away from beneath his, and for the
briefest moment Angus reconsidered his decision.

He'd never be this close again to the fortune she'd offered him. Would he regret it some day? Was living a lie
for twelve months really all that bad given such a massive
payday?

And a second consideration snuck into his subconscious.
Or maybe he should just do this for Ivy?

Angus straightened in his chair, subtly putting further
distance between them.

No. He wouldn't regret passing on the money. His parents had taught him the value of hard work and, in every
aspect of his life, he'd never been one to take shortcuts.

And for Ivy?

No. That was a slippery slope he did not want to get

on. When he was deployed, he never allowed himself to clutter his mind with those he left behind. It was why he would never marry, and it was why he had never meant to have children. It wasn't fair to anyone to be shoved aside in that manner. But it was what he did. It was, quite simply, who he was.

So no, he wasn't going to do this for Ivy.

'I'm sorry, I don't feel like eating,' Ivy said, breaking the silence. She pushed her chair backwards a little quickly, and steadied it with one hand as she stood.

Angus followed her lead and pulled himself to his feet, more than keen to get out of the bar. Around them, other couples and small groups appeared to be enjoying their meals. A man reached out to stroke the cheek of his date. Four well-dressed young women suddenly cackled with laughter and clinked their wine glasses together.

Everyone else's lives appeared to be carrying on beautifully, and normally, and yet Angus's life had just irrevocably changed for ever.

It still didn't seem possible. Didn't seem real.

Ivy was already negotiating all the happy diners, and Angus needed to take several large strides to catch up with her. Automatically, he reached out and rested his hand in the small of her back.

At his touch, she went still, her chin shooting up as she met his gaze.

She'd done a poor job hiding the sheen to her eyes back at the table, and she was far less successful now. Again her gaze was more than wobbly, and he was reminded that he wasn't alone in his shock and disbelief.

He felt he should say something. Something reassuring and supportive.

But he didn't have any experience in this kind of thing. Hell, his ex-girlfriends had made it clear he was a complete failure at even the most simple of relationships—let alone what to say to the woman who had just announced she was carrying his child.

So he said nothing at all, and Ivy's gaze just kept on wobbling.

'Ivy!'

Against his palm, Angus felt Ivy tense.

At the bar, only a few metres away, sat a seriously glamorous blonde. Her hair tumbled in generous waves over one shoulder, and beside her was a significantly less glamorous man.

Ivy appeared struck dumb, and didn't move a millimetre as the pair approached them.

'It's been months!' the blonde exclaimed. 'How are you?'

'I—uh—' Ivy began, and then went silent, simply sending him a panicky glance. Her body was moving now. She was trembling.

Immediately Angus slid his hand from her back to her waist, and tugged her gently against him. Even now, when he shouldn't, he noticed how naturally she fitted against him. And how soft and warm her body felt.

'I'm Angus Barlow,' he said to the couple, offering his free hand.

Then for the next three minutes he scrounged every last ounce of charm he possessed to conduct the most trivial of conversations, while Ivy managed the occasional nod and single-word response. And then he politely excused them, and escorted Ivy outside as quickly as their legs would carry them.

Outside, the night was cool against his skin. His arm was still around Ivy, and in the cold it seemed illogical to remove it, given the flimsiness of her dress.

He was still walking briskly, keen to put as much space between himself and the bar, when Ivy came to an abrupt stop and disentangled herself from him.

'Where are you going?' she said.

Angus paused. His car was parked in the opposite direction.

'I have no idea,' he said.

And amongst all that had happened tonight, those four little words were suddenly hilarious, and he burst into a harsh bark of laughter.

A moment later, Ivy joined in, and they both stood together on the footpath, cackling away just like those women having dinner.

When they both fell silent, Ivy looked up at him again.

No wobbles this time, just direct, real Ivy.

'Thank you,' she said.

CHAPTER FOUR

IVY LISTENED HALF-HEARTEDLY to her sisters' enthusiastic gossip. They sat across from her, their finished breakfast plates pushed aside. To her left sat Ivy's mother, nursing a mug full of cappuccino.

Around them, Sunday morning at the exclusive beach-side café was a buzz of activity. Ivy found herself picking up random snippets of conversation: the waiter two tables to her right repeating an order; an older man complaining at the lateness of his grandson; and from somewhere behind her a high-pitched: *Really?* followed by raucous laughter.

Their table abutted a wall of bi-fold windows, their lou-vred glass panes opened to welcome the salty breeze. Beneath them, keen sunbathers lay on brightly coloured towels in an irregular patchwork. It was an unusually warm October day, and Cottesloe Beach was, it seemed, the place to be.

It had worked out perfectly, really. Her family—just Mila, April and her mother—had dinner every second Sunday. But this weekend she'd suggested breakfast instead, so here they were.

The weather would be perfect for it! she'd said.

And everyone agreed.

As lies went, it was very much the whitest of them, but it still sat so uncomfortably. All to avoid refusing a glass of wine.

She was so close to her sisters, as different as they were. Mila, with her chocolate-brown curls and brilliant smile, was the baby, and the family artist. Never much interested in study, she'd barely finished high school before beginning a string of courses at TAFE—jewellery design, dress making, and a few others that Ivy had long forgotten. But then she'd started—and this time finished—a pottery course, and that was it. Mila had found her calling. Now she had her own studio, with a shop front for her work out the front, and space for her to teach out the back. Quiet, but opinionated and wise, Mila could always be counted on to see through the crap in any situation.

Then there was April. Beautiful, clever but flighty, she'd been the real rebel. She'd partied through uni, and still partied now. She'd completed her Environmental Science degree—chosen for its not so subtle dig at the way her family had made their fortune—but, apart from a few internships, hadn't settled into full-time work. April brought sunshine wherever she went—always the first to smile and the first with a kind word.

And there she was. Ivy. The eldest by three years, she'd followed the script exactly as her mother had hoped: a diligent student throughout school. A top student at university, all the way through to her masters. Then straight to work for the family company, working her way up, just as her mother had, with, of course, a healthy dose of expected nepotism.

But Ivy knew she deserved her position at Molyneux Mining. She'd worked her butt off to get there.

So, yes. In contrast to her arty sister, and her partying sister, there she was: studious, perfect daughter Ivy. Mila and April even gave her well-deserved needling for it.

But, of course, it had never been entirely true.

Ivy knew that. Her mother knew that. But no one else did.

Her mother had fixed her mistakes of more than a decade ago.

Unfortunately, Ivy was no closer to fixing her latest mistake.

She just needed time.

She *would* tell them about her pregnancy. Soon.

Just not today.

'Earth to Ivy?' April was grinning at her, fun sparkling in her gaze. 'You still with us?'

Ivy blinked, and forced a smile. 'Sorry. Just thinking about an email I have to write when I get home for the Bullah Bullah Downs project.'

In unison, her sisters groaned.

'I was just saying that I saw Holly at the shops yesterday,' April said, with a grin. 'She had some *very* interesting news.'

Ivy went perfectly still, pasting on a faux smile. She had the fleeting, horrifying thought that somehow she'd forgotten blurting out the news of her pregnancy to Holly as she'd exited the bar on Thursday night.

'*Apparently*,' April continued, 'you were with a rather hot guy?'

So Evan hadn't told April she'd asked for Angus's number. She could barely remember the vague, somehow work-related excuse she'd given her brother in law, but apparently it had been plausible.

'Oh, he was a blind date,' Ivy said, with a dismissive smile. 'He was nice enough, but it was a bit of a disaster, really.' That was true, in a way. 'No spark, you know?'

Definitely a lie.

The conversation moved on, her mum and sisters familiar enough with her occasional forays into dating to accept what she'd said.

But Ivy remained silent, quietly furious with herself.

She couldn't have news of her pregnancy leaked until she was one hundred per cent prepared, and gossipy speculation about her and Angus would not help that cause.

She needed to be more careful.

And more importantly, she really needed to fix this. Soon.

'Gus! How are you, mate?'

Angus finished the last two repetitions of the set, then swivelled on the seat of the leg press to grab his towel. Cam Dunstall wore his own towel hung over his shoulders, but he clearly hadn't begun his workout as he was the only person in the crowded barracks gym not coated in a layer of sweat.

'Good,' Angus said automatically.

Cam's attention darted to his still-bandaged right wrist. 'Going okay?'

Angus smiled at his friend's obvious concern. They both knew if his wrist was busted, so was his SAS career. He wasn't much use if he couldn't use a firearm.

'Nah, it's no big deal,' he said, truthfully. 'I met with the specialist today. He's happy with my progress. He sees no reason why I shouldn't be back on deck within the month.'

Cam's smile was broad and relieved. 'Awesome news, mate. Hey, you missed out on some fun last week—middle of the night hanging out of a Black Hawk chopper. Good times.'

Cam then went into great detail about the training exercise, while Angus mopped his face and arms of sweat. He'd finished today's workout. In fact he'd been here for the couple of hours since his doctor's appointment.

The good news about his wrist was not unexpected. To be honest, his hand felt very near to normal now—if the doctor had let him he'd already be back at work.

So his workout was supposed to be the highlight of his day. It was Monday, four days since Ivy had dropped her bombshell.

On Friday he'd gone for a run instead, needing to be outside.

Then on the weekend he'd stayed at home, deciding that

cutting back two huge branches from the towering blue gum in what was once his mother's back garden was the best use of his time. But even two days wielding a chain-saw hadn't helped.

And today hadn't helped either.

He still didn't feel normal. The exercise high he craved eluded him.

It wasn't fair.

That made him smile. Out of all that had happened, the incredible bad luck that had plonked him and Ivy in this situation—*that* was what was unfair?

'Mate?' Cam was looking at him strangely. 'I was just asking if you'd heard that Patrick has been moved. To *train-ing*.'

Ah. A smile was certainly not appropriate here. That was no promotion.

'He's still not right, then?' Angus asked, knowing that was probably the wrong way to phrase his question, but at a loss to come up with something better.

'Yeah. That post-traumatic crap. Like Tom, I guess.'

Like Tom.

Guilt lowered Angus's gaze momentarily. How long since he'd called him? They'd come through SAS selec-tion together seven years ago. Tom—strong, confident, supportive, *brave* Tom. His closest mate. The best sol-dier he knew.

Or at least, he had been.

'Some of the boys are going out for a beer tonight. Want to come?'

Cam was clearly keen to move the conversation on.

Angus got that.

But he shook his head. No. Ivy had texted him earlier, and he was meeting her for a coffee.

Not that he told Cam that, but the other man jumped to

the approximately right conclusion anyway, giving him crap about choosing a girl over his mates.

So Angus laughed and let the words roll off him, wishing like hell they were true.

'Thanks for meeting me.'

Angus raised an eyebrow as he slid into the fifties-style café booth. 'This isn't a business meeting, Ivy.'

She shook her head. 'No, of course not.'

It was just easier for her to think of it like that. She'd even prepared for this *meeting*, in a way. Mentally determining an agenda of items to cover, so that this could be over as efficiently as possible.

She was sure Angus would appreciate that, too.

Quick, efficient and over quickly. A good plan.

'So, I've got a couple of points I'd like to discuss, and I'll start with the most important. Do you intend to be a part of our child's life, and if so, to what extent?'

Angus didn't even blink at her directness. 'I intend to be the best father I can be,' he said. 'Which means I want to be a huge part of their life.'

Ivy nodded sharply. It was the answer she'd expected, although she couldn't exactly say why. She was pleased, though. She'd never been close to her own father. 'Excellent. Okay, so the next point is—'

'Hold it there.' Angus glanced at the coffee she'd downed in the few minutes she'd been waiting for him. 'Now the big question is out of the way, how about I go get us both a coffee, and some cake, and we relax a bit?'

'Relax?'

He grinned. 'Honey, the way I see it we just agreed to another eighteen-odd years to talk about this baby. Why rush things now?'

And with that he stood, and headed for the counter.

Ivy just watched him in somewhat stunned silence as he

made his order, and returned to the table with a number on a chrome stick, which he placed between them.

'I just asked for whatever you had again, plus a selection of cakes as I have no idea what you like. Okay?'

Ivy nodded numbly.

'Great!' he said. 'So, tell me something about yourself.'

'Pardon me?'

He shrugged. 'You heard me.'

Ivy bristled. 'Look, it's great that you're all so fine and relaxed and cool with this, but I don't think you understand how—'

'Ivy,' he said, so firmly that her words froze on her tongue. 'I promise you that I *understand* exactly what is going on here. It's all I've thought about for *four days*. I dreamt about it, even, although I can't say I've spent much time sleeping. I am exhausted, and stressed out of my mind. And frankly, I'm over it. I'm over feeling like that, but I can't do anything about it. Neither can you.'

Ivy's gaze travelled across his face, for the first time noticing the dark circles beneath his eyes and the spidery lines of red in his stare.

He'd just described her weekend, and beneath a thick layer of concealer she even had the matching blackened eyes.

'But we've both decided to do this, so we might as well get to know each other. So again—tell me something about yourself.'

Tell him something?

I'm scared? I don't know what I'm doing? I have *no idea* what to do with you?

'I think that Aussie Rules football is the best game in the whole entire universe.'

And then Angus smiled. A gorgeous smile, an amazing smile.

'So now we have two things in common,' he said.

* * *

A selection of cakes later, Ivy stood with Angus outside the café. It was dark between the street lights, and only the occasional car swished past.

'Where'd you park?' Angus asked.

Ivy shook her head. 'I didn't. I just need to call my driver and he'll come pick me up.'

A sudden gust of wind made her shiver, and Ivy wrapped her arms around herself tightly.

Angus took a step towards her—and for a moment Ivy thought he might put his arm around her again, as he had at the wine bar. But then he didn't, and Ivy took a little longer than she would've liked to decide she was relieved.

Tonight hadn't been as she'd planned. They'd talked about all things unimportant—the favourite football team they shared, the latest movies they'd seen, and even the weather. It *had* been kind of like a date.

Or rather exactly like one. Except it hadn't had that early-date awkwardness. The overenthusiastic laughter or the well-rehearsed anecdotes.

It had been...nice. Better than nice.

'I don't remember—did you ask me to tell you something about myself?'

'No,' Ivy said, smiling. Then added in an obedient sing-song voice: 'So, Angus, tell me something about yourself.'

'I don't leave ladies waiting on the street in the dark. Come on, I'll drive you home.'

Ivy raised her eyebrows. 'What if I live on the other side of the city?'

Angus had already walked a few steps, and looked surprised she hadn't already followed. 'Do you?'

She lived a five-minute drive away. 'No.'

He smiled. 'Well, there you go. But it wouldn't have mattered. I like driving.'

He waited another moment. 'So am I waiting here while you call your driver, or are you letting me drive you home?'

It would take longer to call Simon and wait for him than for Angus to drive her home, and she could think of no good reason to refuse. So she found herself walking beside Angus the short distance to his car, parked around the corner.

It was exactly the type of car she'd expect him to drive: big and black and foreboding. Although its vast size didn't assist with the unexpected sensation of intimacy when the doors were shut and they both sank into the lush leather seats.

Angus didn't switch the radio on, and they sat in silence after she gave him the brief directions to her house.

Now it did feel like a first date. As if they'd just been out for a romantic dinner and Angus were driving her home and they were both wondering if there'd be a kiss on her doorstep.

How sweet. How quaint. How *backwards* given how she and Angus had met.

Ivy dug her nails into her palms, needing to force herself to face reality.

She couldn't let her thoughts wander like this. She needed to focus, to remember what this *really* was.

'I have an estimated due date,' she said, the words sounding brittle in the silence. 'July the second.'

Instantly the atmosphere in the car shifted.

There. Romantic notions *gone.*

'Okay,' Angus said. And Ivy supposed he couldn't say much else.

'That was what we were supposed to talk about today,' she said. 'That's why I wanted to meet. To tell you that I had a scan today, and the baby has measured at five weeks and one day and that it's due on July the second.'

Her words were more jumbled than brittle, now.

'Thank you,' Angus said, and Ivy couldn't interpret his tone at all.

He slowed the car to turn into her driveway. The entrance was gated, but Ivy reached into her handbag for the small remote that swung the gates open.

Angus nosed the car up the long curved driveway and came to a stop before the limestone steps that led to the front door of her rambling nineteen-thirties double-storey home.

An automatic porch light flicked on, but otherwise the house was in darkness.

'No butler to meet you?' Angus asked, although his tone was not pointed, but curious.

Ivy laughed. 'Do you think I have someone feed me grapes as I bathe, too?'

He shrugged. 'You have a driver, so I assumed you had other staff.'

'No,' Ivy said. 'I mean, because of the hours I work I have a weekly cleaner and a regular gardener, but that's it. My home is my sanctuary, and I value my privacy.'

It already felt a little too private in the car, so Ivy opened her door and slid her feet out onto the driveway. She turned to thank Angus for the lift, but he'd climbed out of his seat too, and in a few strides stood beside her at the bottom of the steps.

Ivy didn't know what to do now. Why had he done that? Why hadn't he driven off and escaped while he could?

'So I'm confused. If you value your privacy, why have your driver ferry you to meet me, twice? Where did you tell him you were going?'

'Simon would never intrude on my personal life,' Ivy said.

Although it had taken considerable subterfuge to attend her dating scan today without Simon knowing. In the end, she'd had him drop her off some distance away, and she'd walked to her appointment.

He never would've commented if she'd asked him to drop her off right outside the ultrasound clinic. But really? April and Mila didn't even know yet. She couldn't have her driver find out first, no matter how discreet he might be.

'But regardless,' Angus said, 'wouldn't it just be easier to drive five minutes from your house to meet me?'

He appeared genuinely flummoxed, and Ivy couldn't help but smile. 'Easier, yes—if I had a licence.'

At this he went from flummoxed to stunned. 'How is that possible?'

'I never learnt,' Ivy said. 'Long story.'

And it was. Long and best forgotten.

Ivy turned slightly towards her house. 'So, thanks for the lift, Angus.'

She spoke a little softer than she'd planned, and his name sounded unexpectedly intimate on her lips.

'My pleasure, Ivy,' he said, but totally normally, as if he were talking to the waitress back at the café.

Ivy gave her head a little shake. She was being very, very silly with all these thoughts of dates and doorsteps and softly spoken names.

He'd already started to walk back to the driver's side of the car, so Ivy quickly raced up the steps, the heels of her boots clicking against the stone, and her hand already in her bag, searching for her keys.

But then she heard heavier footsteps on the steps behind her.

'Ivy, wait.'

So she did, key in hand. 'Yes?'

Angus took the steps two at a time and soon stood before her. The porch light's glow was soft, but the angles of his face seemed sharper in the mix of light and shadows.

'Were you okay today?' he asked. 'At the scan?'

Ivy blinked, and her throat felt suddenly tight.

'Uh, yes,' she said. 'Of course. It was fine. I was fine.'

She'd been beyond nervous. Scared and clueless, but still okay. More okay than she'd expected, actually.

'Good,' he said, with a sharp nod. And with that, he was off back down the steps.

Ivy put her key in the lock, but then found herself turning back to face him. He wasn't in his seat yet; instead he stood inside his opened door, as if he'd been watching her.

'I saw him,' she said. 'Or her. Just a spot at the moment. Or a blob. A cute blob, though.'

Angus nodded, and his lips quirked upwards.

'Goodnight, Ivy.'

'Goodnight, Angus.'

And then he climbed into his car and drove away.

CHAPTER FIVE

IVY HAD JUST broken into the secret stash of dry crackers in her desk's bottom drawer, when her phone rang.

Angus.

When he'd driven away from her place last week, they'd had no further plans to meet. So she'd decided she'd just call him occasionally with details of the baby's progress; after all, it was wise to keep her distance until she'd worked things out.

Yes, she knew at some point she'd need to organise some formal access arrangement or similar. But again, that could take place between their lawyers.

So there was definitely no real need to see him again.

Which was a relief, unquestionably.

Then why was her stomach doing all sorts of odd things?

'Hello?' she said, finally picking up the phone.

'You hungry?'

'Starving,' she said, honestly. 'I'm always starving now.'

Ah. That was what the stomach thing was. She clearly hadn't eaten enough crackers.

'Great. Meet me downstairs in five minutes. I know a great burger place we can go to.'

She had a meeting in twenty minutes, so she couldn't, even if meeting Angus in public again wasn't a terrible idea, anyway.

'Sure,' she said, instead.

Then Angus ended the call, and Ivy called her assistant into her office to rearrange her meeting. Ivy chose to ignore

Sarah's incredulous expression—people shifted meetings for frivolous reasons all the time.

Just not Ivy.

Even so, just over five minutes later her heels were clicking across the terrazzo floor of the Molyneux Tower's foyer. Angus stood against one of the mammoth round pillars that dotted the vast space, and also stopped the thirty-three-floor building from collapsing into St Georges Terrace.

Around him men and women in suits and smart coats flowed past, hurrying to lunch, or coffee or meetings. In contrast, nothing about Angus was hurried.

He'd propped his shoulder against the pillar, his arms crossed loosely before him. He wore jeans that might have once been black, but now were faded to a steel grey. His navy T-shirt fitted snugly, highlighting his width and the muscular strength of his arms, while one booted foot was crossed casually over the other. Every line of his body looked one hundred per cent comfortable. As if, despite the marked difference in his attire from every other person in the building, he fitted here perfectly.

But he didn't.

Here, in contrast to the gloss and shine that was Molyneux Mining, Angus looked *raw*. Strong, and hard and... virile.

Here, he was juxtaposed against Ivy's real life—her reality. It should have been a shock, and it certainly should've bothered her.

It definitely would've if she'd allowed herself to think about it. Or if, in fact, she'd been able to think at all.

But she couldn't. As soon as she'd heard his voice she'd apparently lost all common sense. And the instant she'd stepped out of the lift she'd known he was watching her.

Just like in Bali the weight of his attention was remarkable. Remarkable enough that she wobbled a little on her heels when her gaze met his.

He studied her as she walked towards him. She sensed, rather than saw, his gaze travel along her body, taking in her heels, her charcoal pencil skirt, and the pale pink of her silk blouse. She wore a short, three-quarter-sleeved cream wool coat, but it wasn't because of the cold that she shivered when she came to a stop.

That would be because he'd smiled.

'I have a meeting in forty-five minutes,' she said, instead of smiling back.

Her voice was more prickly than the professional she'd hoped for. An attempt to regain control, maybe.

When had she ever been in control around Angus?

He shook his head, his smile now even broader. 'Ivy, Ivy, Ivy...'

She didn't know what that meant, and her eyes narrowed.

But he didn't give her a chance to speak, instead reaching out to wrap his large hand around hers.

'Come on,' he said. 'We'd better hurry up, then.'

Angus considered letting go of Ivy's hand once they'd stepped outside onto the gusty, skyscraper-lined street.

But then he just didn't. What was the harm, really, of holding a gorgeous woman's hand for a minute?

None he could think of. At least none that bested the satisfaction he was getting from Ivy's rather stupefied, and also rather un-Ivy-like acquiescence.

As much as he liked driven, determined, controlled Ivy, there was something to be said about how she reacted to him. He hadn't forgotten a moment about what had happened between them in Bali, and certainly not the way she had responded to him. It was as if *all* her nerve endings had become focused on where he'd touched her. As if how she felt, and how he made her feel, were all that had mattered.

It had given him a sense of control—but not. Because there was no doubt that everything Ivy had done was what she'd wanted to do—it was just that instead of focusing on work or responsibilities, she'd been focusing on what felt good. What felt *really* good.

So it had felt natural to grab her hand today. To stop her beginning another unnecessarily professional and awkward conversation between them. Because he'd known his touch would shut her up.

What he'd forgotten was the impact of her touch on *him*.

Which was why he'd considered dropping her hand as they'd stepped outside.

Considered, then dismissed.

Because touching Ivy felt pretty damn good.

And triggered some pretty damn *amazing* memories. Of naked skin that glowed in the moonlight. Of the glide of her body against his. The sound she'd made when he'd finally slid inside her...

They were at the burger bar.

Angus dropped her hand, and Ivy put space between them, not meeting his gaze.

'There's a table free at the back,' he said, spotting it amongst the lunch-time rush.

With barely a nod, Ivy walked over while Angus grabbed a couple of menus.

Soon after they'd ordered, and Ivy sat with her water glass cupped in both hands, waiting.

She might just as well have spoken: *Get to the point, Angus.*

It was tempting to do the opposite, as he had in that café. To force her to slow down. To just talk without purpose for a minute or as long as they liked.

But his body was still heated from the simple touch of her hand and those not so simple memories.

And seeing Ivy today was about the future, not the past.

'Have you told anyone?' he asked.

'No,' she said, studying him almost cautiously. 'Why?'

'Because I'd like to tell someone.'

Her eyes widened. *'Why?'* And then, *'Who?'*

She looked so shocked he had to smile. 'My mother, and for the usual reason I tell her things—I'd like her to know.'

'Oh,' she said. 'I suppose I hadn't thought you'd want to tell anyone now. It's still so early.'

Yes. His late-night Googling had taught him a lot more than he'd ever thought he'd need to know about pregnancy.

Ivy's gaze had dropped to the table. She'd abandoned her water to fiddle with a napkin, weaving the paper between her fingers. 'Can you wait?' she said. 'I...' a long, long pause '...I need more time.'

Angus almost told her why it didn't really matter when he told his mother. He could've told her yesterday and it was almost impossible she'd remember today. Most weeks, he was lucky if she remembered his name, let alone that he was her son.

But then Ivy would wonder why he'd asked her permission at all.

Angus wasn't entirely sure himself, beyond a sense that it was the right thing to do.

Ivy had raised her gaze again, and she met his, waiting impatiently for his response.

'Okay,' he said, with some reluctance.

When he visited his mother—at least a couple of times a week whenever he was home—he talked. Talked more than he'd talked all week, about anything and everything.

Because that was how he remembered his mother: talking. Once she could've talked the ear off anything and anyone, revelling in her ability to draw remarkable stories out of the most random of people: the girl at the checkout, the elderly man at the park, the parking officer issuing her a ticket...

So silence in her presence made Angus excruciatingly uncomfortable. And while, like his father, he was *not* one to ever talk for the sake of it, when he visited his mother, he did.

And he told her everything. Partly because he did actually want to tell her, but mainly because he desperately needed to fill the space around them both with words.

He'd visited her yesterday, and omitting Ivy and the baby from his monologue had felt like a lie of omission.

Stupid, really, given she'd never know. Really stupid.

Lunch arrived, and for a few minutes they both ate in as much silence as was possible when eating burgers stacked high with gourmet ingredients.

Ivy had been visibly relieved when he'd agreed with her, but the atmosphere between them had changed.

'I thought that after the twelve-week scan would be a good time for us to formalise arrangements,' she said suddenly, a tomato-sauce-tipped chip in her hand. 'Then we can both be free to share the news appropriately.'

Formalise? Appropriately?

Angus gritted his teeth. *Really? This again?*

'Haven't we got beyond this, Ivy? This isn't a business deal. This is our child.'

Ivy put the chip back down on her plate, untouched.

'Of course,' she said. 'But I find it's easier if everything's in writing. Then we won't have any more misunderstandings like today.'

'I wouldn't call today a misunderstanding,' Angus said. 'I'd call it a conversation.'

Ivy raised an eyebrow. 'Hmm.'

She pushed her plate away, although it still held half her lunch.

'I thought you were starving?' he asked.

'I was wrong,' she said. 'I need to get back to that meeting.'

Angus checked his watch. 'You still have fifteen minutes.'

She hooked her handbag over her shoulder, the motions rushed and tense.

'I have to make a phone call I forgot about.' A pause while her gaze flicked out towards the busy street. 'Sorry.'

She was clearly running away, and Angus was not about to chase after her. She reached into her handbag, but Angus stopped the movement with a pointed look.

'I'll cover it,' he said.

Ivy nodded, another agitated movement.

Then she was gone, walking as fast as she could in those towering heels.

And Angus sank back in his chair, leisurely enjoyed the rest of his lunch and wondered what on earth to do with Ivy.

It's better this way.

Ivy nodded sharply to herself as she sat alone in the VIP Lounge at the Perth Airport charter terminal.

It is.

Simple. Uncomplicated. Straightforward.

Sensible.

Why she hadn't thought of it in the first place was beyond her.

Her lawyer had couriered the contract to Angus this morning. Its intent was simple: from now on, all communications between them would be via their lawyers, and they both agreed to keep the pregnancy secret until mutually agreed to in writing. Plus, of course, Angus would receive a generous lump sum on signing.

Now she really didn't need to see Angus again.

Which was *such* a relief.

And necessary.

Because what had she been thinking when he'd called a few days ago? In the same breath that she'd acknowledged to herself that meeting with him so publicly was a terrible idea, she'd cancelled a meeting to do just that.

And of *course* Angus had been noticed in the Molyneux Tower foyer, but she'd been too swept up in...in whatever stupid hormonal thing that Angus did to her that she hadn't cared.

By the time she'd returned from lunch the office had been full of gossipy murmurs. No one was silly enough to ask her about Angus directly, of course—not that that made any difference.

Why had she let him hold her hand?

And how did she fail to consider that Angus may want to tell people?

Her behaviour when it came to Angus Barlow made no sense, and more importantly—it was dangerous. She needed to protect herself, and her child. Hadn't she learnt all those years ago how foolish it was to allow how she felt to guide her decisions?

Back then, she'd lost herself amongst her silly, fanciful ideas about love, and she'd vowed never to let that happen again.

Now she dated appropriate men. Men who were a good match for her life and her career.

Certainly not men who made her skin tingle and her heart race.

If, after the tragic events of all those years ago, she needed a reminder that her decision was for the best—well, this was it.

From the moment Angus had watched her walk down that aisle, she'd got just about everything wrong.

Today, that fat contract with Angus had put things right.

Angus might not like it, but it was for the best.

Ivy stood up, walking over to the small coffee station in the corner of the room. Two walls of the lounge were almost entirely windows, offering her a floor-to-ceiling view of the runways. She was at the northern end of the airport, but the main public domestic and international terminals were close by, so large passenger jets dotted the landscape—both on the tarmac and in the cerulean sky.

The Molyneux Mining jet sat patiently in front of her, and Ivy expected one of the flight attendants would come and collect her shortly.

This trip to Bullah Bullah Downs was just what she needed. It had meant a bit of schedule reshuffling, but it would be worth it. Maybe there, amongst the million-odd acres of space the station stretched across, she'd feel more like herself again.

Her stomach growled, and Ivy glanced downwards, surprised to see her hand resting on her still-flat stomach.

'Ivy.'

Ivy spun around, recognising that deep voice instantly.

'What are you doing here?'

She'd tried to keep her voice calm, but failed miserably, her words all high pitched.

Angus stood in front of the closed door to the lounge, a backpack slung over his shoulder. He wasn't leaning against anything this time, but he still managed that lackadaisical *thing* he did, every inch of his lean frame all easy and relaxed.

Except for his jaw. That had a harder line than usual.

And his eyes.

His eyes… Ivy didn't know how to describe them, she just knew that as he walked—casually—towards her, they were all that she could look at.

Today they didn't have that sexy sparkle of green amongst the hazel…they were just…*flat*.

Even when she'd told him she was pregnant, he hadn't looked like this.

'So, where are we off to, today, Ivy?'

'Pardon me?'

Angus folded himself into the chair Ivy had been sitting in earlier, casually leaning backwards and crossing his feet at the ankles.

'You heard me,' he said. 'I made an educated guess of our destination, so I suspect I've packed appropriately regardless. But still. I'm just plain curious.'

'Packed?'

He nodded, raising his eyebrows. 'Now, this is one thing I haven't read about in early pregnancy: hearing loss. Interesting.'

Ivy's gaze narrowed, her brain rapidly recovering from the shock of Angus's sudden appearance.

'You're not coming with me,' she said.

While she might have worked that out, she had no clue why on earth he would want to. *What was going on?*

'Of course I am,' he said. 'Your very helpful assistant advised that you would be unavailable for the next three days, which is unacceptable to me. So here I am.'

'Nothing I do needs to be acceptable, or otherwise, to you,' Ivy said, with some venom.

He nodded again, the action utterly infuriating. 'Oh, yes, it does, Ivy. I think that's the bit you forgot when you spoke to your lawyer. Your disregard for our agreement *not to tell anybody* is remarkable.'

Ivy crossed her arms in front of herself. 'I had to tell my lawyer.'

'No,' Angus said, softer now. 'You didn't.'

Ivy bit her lip. He was right, and she wasn't sure the fact that she really hadn't wanted to would make Angus any happier.

'I've realised that it would be better to formalise things sooner rather than later. Neither of us meant this to happen, and although I appreciate how nice you've been so far—' Angus raised an eyebrow when she said *nice* '—there really is no need for it. I can keep you updated on the baby's progress via my lawyer, and we can organise an access arrangement for after the baby's birth.'

'Yes,' Angus said. 'I noticed that part in the contract—organised between our lawyers, of course.'

Ivy nodded. 'Yes. That way we have everything in writing. Nice and clear.'

'And you don't have to see me.'

Angus stood up, and in three large strides was right in front of her. Close enough that it took everything in Ivy not to take a step backwards.

'We don't have to see *each other*,' Ivy clarified. She held Angus's gaze as he looked at her, but it was hard. It was as if he was attempting to look beyond her eyes—to work out what she was thinking.

Unfortunately with Angus so close, what she was thinking was nothing particularly coherent at all. Which was, of course, the problem. She just couldn't allow this—this pointless, hormone-triggered *reaction* to him.

'But what if I like seeing you, Ivy?' he said. Deliberately he swept his gaze along her body, from her hair to her toes, and slowly back up again. She was dressed for the flight in skinny jeans and a fine wool long-line jumper. Hardly her most glamorous outfit, and yet she still felt the appreciation in his gaze. Felt that *weight*.

'I—' Ivy began, but really had no idea what she was trying to say.

'Ms Molyneux?'

The voice came from the doorway. A male flight attendant in his perfectly ironed uniform waited patiently, his expression curious.

'We'll just be a minute,' said Angus, and Ivy glared at him.

'We?' the attendant asked. 'Ms Molyneux, should we have the paperwork for your guest?'

Ivy shook her head, but said nothing.

Angus leaned close, so only Ivy could hear him. 'I am going to be a part of this child's life, Ivy, and that means being a part of yours—and *not* through a lawyer. This is the second time this week you've run away from me, Ivy, and I don't like it.'

'I don't run away from things,' Ivy said, low but firm.

'Don't you?' he said, taking a step back. 'What would you call this?'

'Work,' she said. 'Besides, how would I explain who you are?'

Angus's lips quirked into a smile of triumph.

Ivy closed her eyes and counted to ten. Slowly. More than once.

'Fine,' she said, when she looked at him again. She turned to the still-waiting attendant. 'Louis—please organise the appropriate paperwork with Mr Barlow.'

Then, with a resigned sigh, she went to collect her laptop and handbag from the coffee table as Angus left the room.

Alone again, Ivy looked back out to the runway. Her plane still waited patiently for her, but the sky beyond had turned from a perfect blue to an ominous grey. Appropriate.

Her stomach growled, but the platter of plastic-wrapped cookies at the tea and coffee station suddenly held no appeal. Instead she watched the trajectory of a passenger jet across the gloomy sky as she struggled to get her thoughts back in order and work out what on earth she was going to do next.

But it was a pretty impossible task.

As with everything that had happened with Angus until now, Ivy had absolutely no idea what she was doing.

CHAPTER SIX

Two HOURS LATER the plane touched down at Paraburdoo airport.

For the entire flight, Ivy had sat stiffly across from Angus, appearing remarkably uncomfortable despite her luxurious leather seat. She'd spent much of her time busily typing away on her laptop, only occasionally taking a break to stare out of the window.

It was quite a view, too. In Perth, the landscape had been in shades of green, but as they'd travelled north it had transformed into a world of browns and ochres, patterned with deep cuts and ridges—some the ancient gorges of Karijini National Park and others the brutal gash of an iron ore mine.

Unlike Ivy, Angus had enjoyed his time aboard the Cessna. He'd chosen a European beer from the extensive bar, and worked his way through a good portion of the cheese platter placed before them.

The silence hadn't bothered him; he knew—with the pilot and Louis nearby—it had not been the time to talk.

At the airport, the heat buffeted them the moment they exited the jet. Perth in October was quite mild, still a good few months from summer. But here in the Pilbara it never really got cold—at least not during the day—and today the temperature was well into the thirties.

The airport was busy—a hub for all of the iron-ore companies ferrying their fly-in/fly-out workers from the city. Even with only a single runway, it had a decent terminal, today filled with men and women in high-visibility cloth-ing and steel-capped work boots.

Outside, a car waited for them. A hulking white four-wheel drive with a substantial bull bar, an oversized aerial and an air snorkel, it was far from a limousine—and yet there he was, the driver, waiting beside the front wheel for them.

'Do you know how to get where we're going?' Angus asked Ivy as they walked to the car.

'Of course,' she said. 'I've been coming here my whole life.'

'Then tell him he's not needed.'

Ivy stopped dead. 'Pardon me?'

'There it is again, that early pregnancy hearing loss.'

Ivy's lush lips formed into a very thin line.

Angus sighed. 'We don't need a driver. I can drive.'

Her mouth opened and closed a few times, as if she was searching for the perfect argument.

'If he drives, I'll talk about the baby all the way there.'

Ivy's eyes widened. 'That's blackmail.'

Angus shrugged. But then, Ivy had stopped playing nice when she'd had that contract couriered to him.

He wasn't surprised when Ivy walked ahead to speak to the driver. Minutes later, the other man was gone, and Angus was in the driver's seat, Ivy belted in beside him.

She tapped away at the GPS embedded in the dashboard.

'There,' she said. 'Follow this. I'm going to take a nap.'

Then she turned slightly away from him in her seat, and firmly closed her eyes.

Angus didn't believe for a second that she was actually going to sleep, but he didn't argue.

They had two days ahead of them to talk, if necessary. He was in no hurry.

* * *

'Ivy?'

Ivy blinked sleepily. A large hand cupped her shoulder, shaking her gently.

'We're here. But it doesn't look much like an iron-ore mine.'

Slowly her eyes focused. The car's windows were coated in a thin layer of red dust, thanks to the kilometres of unsealed roads they'd travelled along to arrive at their destination. Fifty-seven kilometres north east of Paraburdoo, Bullah Bullah Downs homestead sat silently against a backdrop of yellow-flowering cassias and acacia trees and amongst a tufty carpet of spinifex in greens and blueish grey. The building was old, originally built in the early nineteen-twenties, but renovated extensively on the inside by Ivy's mother multiple times over the past thirty years.

The homestead's red tin roof was exactly the same shade as the soil it was built upon, reaching out to create a veranda to encircle itself. The walls were solid stone, the mortar rough and ready.

It was remote, it was arid, and it was *home*. In many ways more like home than the mansion in Dalkeith where Ivy had grown up.

Ivy loved it here. Despite everything, and despite having Angus Barlow beside her, she smiled.

She'd slumped against the side of the car as she'd slept, and Ivy now straightened up, stretching out her legs.

The road out here was mostly dirt and studded with pot holes. How she'd slept was beyond her, and it hadn't been intentional. She'd planned to just close her eyes and buy some time before she and Angus spoke.

Buy some time to do what, she wasn't exactly sure.

'Where are we?' Angus asked.

'The homestead,' Ivy said as she opened her door and

pivoted in her seat to climb out. 'Come on, I'll give you a tour.'

Keen to get inside, Ivy jumped from the car, but the instant her feet touched red dirt she knew something was very, very wrong.

Patches of white flashed into her vision, blocking the homestead, and blocking Angus when she instinctively turned to him.

'Angus?' she began, but that was all she could manage before everything went black.

'Ivy?'

Everything was still black. Something coated her lips, so Ivy took an experimental lick.

Dirt.

Yuk.

Her eyes sprung open. Immediately in front of her was the deeply corrugated tread of a four-wheel drive tyre. She was on her side, her legs bent, her arms laid out in front of her.

Ivy knew enough from basic first-aid training to know she was in the recovery position.

'I fainted,' she said.

'Just for a few seconds,' Angus said from where he knelt behind her. 'Enough time to freak me out.'

The remnants of that sudden dizziness remained, so for now Ivy didn't move.

'Freak you out?' Ivy said. 'Surely a simple faint isn't going to ruffle a soldier?'

Angus's laugh was low. 'I suppose you'd expect a soldier to catch you, too.'

'You didn't?' she asked, surprised, although now she registered a dull ache in her hip and she could see a few grazes on her arms, tiny pinpricks of blood decorating her skin. 'You're right,' she said with a smile, 'I am disappointed.'

'One moment you were there, then I heard the thud as you hit the ground. Thank God you didn't hit the car or a rock.' He paused. 'Has this happened before?'

'No,' she said. 'Although I have felt a bit nauseous if I don't eat regularly.'

'You didn't eat on the plane,' Angus said. 'So it's been at least three hours.'

'Yeah,' Ivy said. 'I was too grumpy during the flight to eat.'

She must still be dizzy; it wasn't like her to be quite so candid.

Angus laughed out loud. 'Grumpy with me or not, promise me you won't go so long between eating again.'

Ivy's automatic reaction was to tell Angus she was a grown woman perfectly capable of feeding herself. In fact, she rolled onto her back to tell him exactly that—but then met his gaze.

And it wasn't flat any more. It wasn't anything like it had been back in the VIP Lounge, or on the plane, and definitely not the ruthless stare he'd maintained when he had demanded she send her driver away.

The flecks of green were back in his eyes, and all she could see was concern.

Big, bad, brave soldier or not, she had scared him.

So those sharp words stuck in her throat.

'When we get inside, I want you to call your doctor.'

Ivy nodded obediently.

'Feeling faint is common in early pregnancy, but even so I'd feel better if you discussed this with a professional.'

She nodded again. 'You've done more research than me,' Ivy said.

He shrugged. 'I believe in being prepared.'

'Except when making love on the beach,' she teased.

Ivy had absolutely no idea where that came from, and instantly her cheeks went scalding hot.

But Angus laughed again. 'Maybe a bit too early for that joke, Ivy?'

'Probably,' she agreed, but her blush was fading.

Fainting was almost worth it to hear him laugh. To see that sparkle back in his gaze.

'How you doing now?' Angus said. 'Do you think you'll be able to walk to the house?'

'Of course,' she said, levering her upper body off the ground.

'Not so fast,' he said, and then in a smooth, effortless motion, he scooped her up. With a powerful, warm arm beneath her knees, and another encircling her back, it was momentarily impossible to talk. He held her close, her head nestled against his shoulder. He smelt fantastic: clean and strong. Instinctively she curled closer, wanting to be as close as possible to all that heat and strength.

In the shade of the veranda, finally Ivy's voice returned.

'Why did you ask if I could walk if you were always going to carry me?'

'Because I like it when things don't go the way you expect.'

She had a feeling she should be offended, but a combination of sun, dizziness and Angus's befuddling proximity meant she was in no position to mount a defence.

And with that, he carefully placed her back on her feet, a supportive arm remaining around her waist.

With his free arm he gave Ivy her handbag, liberally covered in dust.

In silence she found the key, unlocked the front door, and, with Angus's arm still close around her, led them inside.

The homestead's lounge room was something else. Angus couldn't imagine the room had even a passing resemblance to the decorating of the early nineteen-hundreds, but it was certainly beautiful. The floors were polished jarrah, the leather couches oversized and comfortable. Above the cast-iron fireplace a huge mirror reflected the view—although now it was dusk the undulating landscape's shades of red and splashes of green were muted. Elaborately patterned curtains edged the windows, and a thick-pile rug lay beneath their feet.

Air conditioning ensured the temperature inside was perfect, which Angus was grateful for as he studied Ivy.

She lay stretched out on the couch, her gaze trained at the ceiling. She'd had a shower to wash away all that red dust, and now she wore a loose singlet and yoga pants, her wet hair looped into a ponytail.

She insisted she was fine, but still—he worried.

He didn't think he'd ever forget the sound of Ivy's body thudding against the red earth.

Amongst so many—objectively far worse—memories that crammed his head, it was strange that he was so sure of that fact. But he was.

And he couldn't even say it was just about their baby. In fact, it wasn't until she finally opened her eyes—and it had felt like hours, not seconds—that he even thought about him or her.

Was that bad?

He propped his elbows on his knees, rubbing his hand against his forehead.

Probably.

Slowly, Ivy pulled herself to a seated position.

'Careful!' he said, automatically.

She responded with a glare. 'I am not an invalid. Even my doctor gave me the all-clear.'

'As long as it doesn't happen again.'

She sighed. 'It won't.' She gestured at the half-eaten box

of crackers and the remaining wedge of Cheddar cheese on the coffee table. 'I am suitably fortified, I promise.'

But still, he watched warily as she crossed the room to the adjacent kitchen. She walked slowly—he suspected mostly for his benefit—and made it to the fridge in one piece.

On cue, she threw her arms out with a flourish, and took a theatrical bow in his direction. 'Waa-*lah*! Behold! The amazing walking woman!'

Angus didn't even bother to raise an eyebrow, although he couldn't help his halfway smile.

Somehow they had fallen into a truce. A demilitarised zone of sorts.

But this wasn't what he had planned—this rather cosy scene in such a luxurious setting.

But then, he'd expected they would talk in a meeting room at a mine site. As it turned out, the three Bullah Bullah Downs mines were located many, many kilometres away from the homestead, and when he'd asked Ivy said she'd had no plans to visit them.

So he had been right. Ivy had run away to Bullah Bullah Downs. She'd quite literally sent the contract, and run.

And while a big portion of him was incredibly angry at her behaviour, all he saw as Ivy walked towards him with an overflowing platter in her arms was how she'd looked, crumpled on the ground beside the car.

Fragile. Vulnerable.

Not that she'd appreciate him thinking that. And Angus didn't really think it was true. Ivy was strong, Ivy was independent.

But she was also pregnant, and for reasons he didn't fully comprehend—she was scared.

'I may have gone overboard in my attempt to divert any hint of a rumour,' Ivy said, putting the platter down on the coffee table. 'So please enjoy your sushi and selection of soft cheeses. There's also a *lot* of wine in the fridge.'

Angus leant forward to study the feast. 'And I see you aren't about to starve, though.'

'No,' Ivy said with a smile. 'Hard cheeses, bread and nuts seem to be my thing at the moment. And apples. And cake. There are actually quite a few cakes in the fridge. I may have been a little overenthusiastic when I made my catering order, too.' She paused. 'I suspect any rumours will instead be in relation to my new-found gluttony.'

For a while they both ate quietly, picking at the decadent food before them.

Tension still simmered between them, but now it wasn't tinged with anger.

Pity he'd have to change that.

'Why did you send me that contract, Ivy?'

Ivy's head jerked up. She put her plate back on the coffee table, and then rearranged her legs from underneath her so she sat primly on the edge of the sofa, rather than comfortably cross-legged amongst the pillows.

'I should've done it to start with.'

'That doesn't answer my question.'

She looked away, staring out through the now darkened window at nothing.

'I felt it was my only option.'

'That doesn't answer it either. Why?'

Her gaze snapped back to meet his, and it was immediately obvious that their truce was over. 'You just don't get it, do you?' she said, jumping to her feet. 'This is so easy for you, while *everything* in my life has to change. It's not fair.'

Just like that, Angus was angry, too.

'This is life-changing for me too, Ivy.'

But she shook her head. 'Don't be ridiculous. I told you what's at stake here. My entire professional career hangs in the balance. Nothing has to change for you.'

Nothing had to change for him?

But before he had a chance to set her straight, Ivy continued, oblivious to his clenched jaw and the frustration running through his veins. 'I don't think you understand that I *have* to fix this. I can't just carry on like it's all okay, and that we'll work it out, because we *won't*. We can't have coffee and lunch and talk about football and cancel meetings and just hope that magically it will all work out. Because it *won't*.'

She was pacing the room, crossing from the couch to the kitchen and back. Her arms were wrapped tight around her, and she didn't look at Angus at all.

He stood up, deliberately blocking her path, needing her to look at him.

Needing the Ivy he knew to be looking him straight in the eye when she spoke.

But she instead stared at a spot somewhere on his chest, her jaw in a stubborn line.

'How does not seeing me at all fix anything, Ivy? That was all I saw in the contract, nothing about your career. Or about how you'll erase what happened between us in Bali.'

Her gaze shot upwards to cling with his. 'I don't want to erase what happened in Bali,' she said softly, then shook her head as if she'd only just realised what she'd said, her cheeks a deep pink. 'I mean, just the bit where I forgot to take my pill that day.' Then her gaze dropped down to her belly, which she covered with her hands. 'Oh, I don't think I meant that either, which makes no sense at all.'

Her fingers rubbed at her eyes, smudging make-up he hadn't even realised she'd put on after her shower.

'Ivy, tell me how the contract fixes anything.'

Her hands fell away. 'It doesn't fix everything,' she said. 'But it fixes *you*.'

'What does that even mean?'

She threw her arms in the air, taking a step backwards

so she could gesture between them. 'It fixes *this*. It fixes me having to see you, having to deal with you being all strong and nice and sexy and *confusing*. I'm not myself when I'm with you. I make poor decisions; I don't think straight; I don't do *anything* right. I can't control anything right now. I can't stop my stupid body fainting. I can't stop eating crackers. I can't stop the fact that my whole world is going to collapse around me once I finally get the guts to *tell* anyone but my lawyer that I'm pregnant.' She took a step towards him, tilting her chin upwards to meet his gaze. 'But I can control *this*. I can stop *this*. It's a start, anyway.'

Then her shoulders slumped, and she went to walk away.

But Angus's hand shot out, wrapping around her upper arm.

'You can't control me, Ivy. You can't control everything, no matter how badly you want to.'

He stepped even closer. Ivy's chest was moving up and down as she took deep breaths, as if trying to pull herself together.

Angus loosened his grip on her arm, letting his hand run down past her elbow to her wrist. Beneath his fingertips, she shivered.

'Are you okay?' he said, suddenly worried. 'Are you cold?'

She laughed, but without humour. 'No, Angus. That's just yet another thing I apparently can't control.'

Ivy's heart felt as if it were beating a billion miles an hour. That seemed to be what it did when Angus was so close to her, doing that strong and sexy thing he did so well.

And her skin shivered too, of course, when he touched her.

He'd gone completely still, which was good. It gave Ivy some chance of pulling herself together. Mortification was attempting to distract her from the immediate sensation of

Angus's touch. Because mortified she should be, for pacing around the homestead, ranting to Angus about things he certainly didn't need to know.

But then his fingers began to move again, and the only thing Ivy could possibly think about was the man standing right in front of her.

'I didn't need to carry you inside today,' he said, his voice low and like velvet.

'You were making a point,' she said. 'About expectations.'

She'd barely needed the prompt. Today had confirmed that Angus Barlow was never going to behave the way she expected—or wanted.

But he shook his head. 'No,' he said. 'At least that was a far secondary consideration. Mostly I just wanted to touch you.'

Ivy closed her eyes as warmth pooled low in her belly.

He was still touching her, his fingers having traced their way back up along her arm, across her shoulder to lightly brush against her exposed collarbone.

His touch was so light Ivy found herself swaying towards him, wanting him to be firmer, wanting to feel more than a hint of his strength and his heat.

She jumped at the sudden weight of his other hand on her hip, and his hand went still, as if allowing her a moment to adjust.

And then that hand was moving too, his thumb exploring the shape of her hipbone, his fingers flaring out to caress the upper slope of her backside.

Then the hand curled around further, to splay across the small of her back. Firm. Hard.

Her eyes still closed, she could suddenly feel his breath against her cheek, then her ear.

'You lose control when you're near me,' he said, so softly.

It was pointless to argue, even if she was capable of it. Instead she simply sighed.

'Ivy, I don't want to be in control around you.'

Her eyes snapped open at the feel of those words against her lips. If she moved even a centimetre, their mouths would touch.

But she didn't have to. The hand on her back pulled her firmly against him, his other hand sliding up to tangle in her still-damp hair.

And then his mouth took hers, and he was kissing her.

Hard and hot and all-consuming.

Out of control. But then, that was hardly unexpected.

Her own arms had managed to make their way to his shoulders, to cling and to wrap behind his neck. He didn't really need her to pull him closer, but she gave it a go, wanting to feel every inch of him plastered against her body.

She kissed him back without restraint, far more so than in Bali. She tasted his tongue, explored his mouth, licked and sucked his lips.

And, *God*, how he kissed her back. He was right, she was never in control around him, but as they kissed he gave her the illusion of control, letting her take the lead, letting her press smaller kisses along his jaw, or break away to change the angle of their lips or choose to take things slow or fast.

But it wasn't real. The moment Angus lost patience with her playfulness she found herself in the air for the second time today, being carried to the couch, and pushed deep into the pillows beneath his delicious weight.

And he kissed her then with intent, his hands inching beneath her singlet, her skin aching for his touch.

Her fingers slid along his spine, digging into the heavy muscles as they explored his breadth and shape. But then they found what they were really after—the hem of his T-shirt—and she got to work pulling the fabric upwards, desperate to feel his naked skin against hers.

She cradled him between her thighs, and it was impossible not to rub her body against that hardness.

Then his fingers made it to her bra, cupping her through the satin and lace, his thumb perfectly rough against her nipple.

But then he went still. Completely still.

'Is it okay for the baby for me to be on top of you? Should we swap?'

He might as well have thrown a bucket of water over them both.

Ivy had frozen when Angus went still, but now she felt as cold as ice, the mention of their baby plunging her back into reality.

How had she let this happen?

She pulled his shirt back down, and shoved both her hands against his shoulders.

'Get off me.'

Instantly he was on his feet. 'Are you okay?'

There they were again, those lovely concerned eyes.

Ivy sat up, pulling her bra and singlet back to where they were supposed to be. She knew she was blushing, could feel it covering pretty much every square inch of her skin.

'I'm going to bed,' she said. 'Take any of the other rooms. They all have fresh linen.'

Then she noticed all the food still out. She grabbed at a random serving platter. 'I'll just put this away first. You can go to bed, though.'

She just wanted him away from her.

'Ivy,' he said. 'What just happened?'

She shook her head. 'I think it's better if we both agree nothing happened, don't you?' She remembered his words from that first coffee. 'You know, we've got eighteen years ahead of us and all that?'

Eighteen years with yet another meaningless night of

sex to try not to think about…which of course, would be all this would've been. No, not a good idea.

Finally she managed to look at him.

He nodded sharply. 'You're right,' he said. 'I'll help you tidy up.'

Then together they put the food away and cleaned up the kitchen.

Very politely, very awkwardly.

Then, just as Ivy began walking up the hallway to her room, Angus spoke.

'I'm not going to sign that contract, Ivy. I'm going to be part of our baby's life, and that means I'm going to be a part of yours. Like it or not.'

She didn't bother turning around. 'I know.'

CHAPTER SEVEN

ANGUS LAY IN his incredibly comfortable king-size bed and stared up at the elaborate ceiling rose above the guest room's elegant chandelier without really seeing it.

He'd had a really good night's sleep.

He'd always been good at sleeping anywhere, and at any time—an essential skill in his career. And he certainly didn't need air conditioning, a fluffy doona and fancy sheets.

There were only two times in his life he remembered being unable to sleep: a couple of weeks ago, when Ivy told him she was pregnant. And the night his father died.

That was it.

He also didn't really dream. He just lay his head on the pillow—or in his swag, or on the ground—and slept. *Boom.* And he slept for however long, and woke up. That was it.

Tom had asked him once if he had bad dreams.

Bad dreams about what they'd seen. What they'd done. What had happened to them. What could've happened to them. What could still happen to them.

Because it turned out Tom had really bad dreams. The type of bad dreams where he woke up soaked in sweat, or where his wife needed to shake him awake.

The type of dreams where sometimes he didn't want to go to sleep.

Sometimes, Angus had said. *Sometimes I have bad dreams.*

And Tom had nodded, and swallowed, and looked so

damn relieved that his mate understood what he was going through that Angus had been glad he'd lied.

But it had been a lie.

Because he didn't have those dreams.

He didn't come home from combat and then feel unsafe in his own home. He wasn't alert to every sound, to every movement.

He didn't sometimes sleep in his lounge room with all the lights on. Or drive all night so he didn't have to sleep at all.

He didn't gamble or drink or do drugs to dull painful memories.

He debriefed, he came home, and he was fine.

But not everyone came home fine. Tom hadn't come home fine. The guy that Cam had told him about—Patrick—he was messed up too.

And Angus knew some of the guys saw psychs at times. It made sense. Most guys seemed to work their way through it, and they'd all been told enough times about normal reactions to trauma that he knew it was just that: *normal.*

Although some guys didn't work through it. Tom hadn't.

But how about him? How about Angus?

How could he be so unaffected? How could he blissfully sleep like a log when he'd experienced so much, *knew* so much?

When your work dealt directly with life and death—and the pendulum could so easily swing one way or the other—*of course* that would mess you up, at least a little?

At some point—before Tom's diagnosis with posttraumatic stress disorder—Angus had been quietly rather proud of his resilience.

He'd thought he was particularly tough. Thought he was particularly strong.

But Tom had been tough, as tough as Angus. Tougher. Stronger.

So now…now he didn't think he should be proud.

Now he wondered what it was he lacked.

Of course it wasn't the same, but wasn't it at least a little unusual that he could have the most explosive kiss of his life with a woman who'd literally turned his life upside down, and then sleep in a strange bed for—he rolled over to check his phone—almost eight hours straight?

Shouldn't he have tossed and turned, just a little?

Yesterday Ivy had tried so desperately to control him—to pack him away into a neat little lawyer-lined box. She didn't like the undeniable pull of attraction between them, that was clear. To be honest, Angus wasn't a big fan, either.

It *did* complicate things.

Last night Ivy had told him she lost control around him, and he'd openly told her that he found it pretty hard to stay in control around her, too.

And that did surprise him. He'd followed Ivy up here because that contract had made him so damn angry—and because he wasn't going to let Ivy manipulate him.

He certainly hadn't intended to kiss her.

He wanted a relationship with his child, and he wanted a cordial relationship with Ivy. Nothing more.

There was a reason he was single now, and his previous girlfriends had all eventually become fed up with him.

He'd begun to join the dots years ago, beginning to see the similarities between his ability to process and shrug off the impacts of war and his ability to distance himself so effortlessly within a relationship.

The thing was, in his job, it was a good thing. In day-to-day life, not so much.

So it was better, he'd decided, simply not to have relationships. That way he didn't hurt anyone. And he certainly didn't want to hurt Ivy.

Angus levered himself up and swung his legs off the

bed. He'd slept in only his boxers, and the air conditioning was cool against his skin.

Last night, when Ivy had yanked up his T-shirt, the air conditioning had been shockingly cold against his heated body—for a moment. But he'd immediately forgotten that when he'd been so absorbed in Ivy and the soft skin of her hips, and belly and breasts...

Angus smiled.

So no, he might not have dreamed of Ivy, or tossed and turned all night.

But it couldn't hurt to think about her now: how she felt, how she'd looked.

The flush to her cheeks, the pink of her lips, how she'd felt so perfect beneath him, even if separated by too many layers of clothes...

The house was silent as Angus walked to the en-suite bathroom for a shower.

He wasn't usually one to daydream, either.

But for Ivy, it would seem he'd made an exception.

Ivy woke up to the smell of cooking bacon.

Mmm. Bacon.

Bacon?

Ivy's eyes popped open. Sun was streaming in through the curtains she'd left open all night, and it was clearly a long time past dawn.

Angus.

She squeezed her eyes shut again.

Angus.

He'd filled her dreams—not for the first time—and he was still here now that she'd woken up.

Not that he could've left. It wasn't as if he could easily flag down a taxi.

But that would've been nice, though. To wake up, and for Angus to have magically disappeared.

That way this weekend could've been what it was supposed to be. A break. A *proper* break, not like every other holiday she could remember.

No work. No nothing. Just—herself, and Bullah Bullah Downs.

Perfect.

But that really wasn't working out, was it?

Nothing was working out right now. *Nothing.*

Not her supposed holiday, not the contract, and not that kiss.

How had she let that happen?

Ivy noticed she'd brought her fingers to her lips and snatched them away. Why had she done that? To test if they felt different? Bruised? Ravished? Special?

They didn't, of course. Because nothing had changed, not really.

What was yet another awkward memory between them?

She climbed out of bed and got dressed. It would be hot today—it always was this time of year. She'd planned to head out to one of the gorges at Karijini today, but without a driver that wouldn't happen. She'd had Martin booked all weekend to come collect her as needed, but she'd been too flustered at the airport to think of only cancelling his initial task of driving her to the homestead.

Instead, she'd organise for the Molyneux jet to fly both Angus and herself home today. It wasn't as if she'd be able to relax this weekend, even once Angus left.

Besides, it would also give her all of Sunday to work.

Dressed in tailored navy-blue shorts and a cream linen tank-top, she headed for the kitchen.

Angus sat on one of the tall stools at the breakfast bar, a full plate of bacon and eggs piled up in front of him.

'I hope you don't mind,' he said, his back to her. 'I may have already started.'

He twisted on his seat, and then paused as he ran his gaze along her body.

'You have great legs,' he said, so matter-of-fact that Ivy blinked. 'I haven't seen that much of them before in daylight.'

At this, she blushed.

He grinned, and left his plate to walk to the other side of the bench. The gas cooktop sat in the middle of all that white-speckled granite, a couple of fry pans already in place.

'How do you like your eggs?'

Ivy still stood, frozen, in the door way. This wasn't what she had expected. She'd expected silence. Possibly antagonism.

Not this. Not a sexy smile, complete with matching sexy stubble.

He stood comfortably in her kitchen. As if he belonged, and as if he had nowhere else to be.

'Scrambled,' she said, eventually, then left the relative safety of the hall to slide onto the stool beside his.

She ate her breakfast almost warily, not at all sure what was going on.

'What are we doing today?' he asked, laying his knife and fork together on his now empty plate.

'I'll phone my office after breakfast and organise for the jet to come pick us up. With any luck we'll be home by late afternoon.'

'Why would you do that?'

Ivy looked up from her eggs, surprised. 'Because you want to go home, and I can't justify the cost of the jet flying up tomorrow as well.'

Angus leant against the low backrest of his stool, and crossed his arms. 'I never said that. I'm happy to stay.'

'You're happy to stay?' Ivy repeated. 'You mean, you're

happy to remain uninvited in my home with me—a woman you don't like very much?'

His lips quirked upwards. 'Oh, I think we both know that isn't true, Ivy.'

Ivy shook her head as her cheeks heated, ignoring him. 'No,' she said, 'I think it's best if we both go home. I was silly to fly up anyway. I have so much work to do—'

'Ivy,' he said firmly. 'I meant it last night. I'm going to be a part of our baby's life, and that does mean being part of yours. Given that, doesn't it make sense we get to know each other better?'

'Didn't we try this before, at the café?' she said. 'Besides, we can talk on the plane if you want. Play twenty questions with each other or something.'

'I'm not getting on a plane today, Ivy. I'm going to drive out to Karijini and explore. I've never been to the national park before—it would be crazy not to go this weekend when we're so close. And I was hoping you'd be my guide.'

His plans were so similar to what Ivy had originally intended, it would've been uncanny—if visiting Karijini and mining iron ore weren't basically the only two things you *could* do in the Pilbara.

Even so, it was tempting.

A big part of her—the stubborn part—wanted to stick to her guns, and insist she absolutely must fly home to work.

But another part of her—the bit that was tired of arguing, and also just plain *tired*—couldn't do it.

She could think of a lot worse things to do today than go swimming in a secluded waterhole amongst plunging gorges two and a half billion years old. And working all afternoon was certainly one of them.

Plus, reluctantly, she had to acknowledge that Angus had a point. If she was stuck dealing with Angus—and she was, now that he wouldn't sign her contract—maybe it would help to spend more—platonic—time together. Maybe familiarity would even dilute the attraction between them.

She could hope, anyway.

'We'll go to Fern Pool,' she said, 'but we need to get moving. It's a decent drive.'

Angus studied her for a long moment, and Ivy liked that she'd clearly surprised him.

Then he smiled, and Ivy found she liked that even better—and couldn't bring herself to care that that probably wasn't a good thing.

'Sounds like a plan,' Angus said. 'Let's go.'

Angus drove them out to Fortescue Falls. The forty-minute drive took them from red gravel to smooth bitumen and back to red gravel again as they approached the car park. October wasn't the best time of year to come to Karijini, with the unrelenting, impossible heat of summer only weeks away, but it did mean far fewer tourists, with only two other cars parked amongst the dirt and the surrounding scrub-tufted hills.

But they were lucky—today was perfect: low thirties with a glorious, cloudless blue sky. At a little hut, Ivy paid the small entry fee, then smiled at Angus over her shoulder as she pointed towards the deep red sand track ahead of them. He wore a black T-shirt, knee-length shorts, leather work boots and a backpack slung over his shoulders—and he looked one hundred per cent like the soldier he was, complete with bulging biceps and muscular calves. Ivy didn't think she'd ever admired a man's calves before. In fact, until today, she wouldn't even have thought it possible that they could be attractive.

But, it turned out, they could. Hair and everything.

It wasn't a long walk to Dales Gorge, less than half a kilometre. Here it was perfectly flat and easy—a stark contrast to the descent ahead of them. Ivy enjoyed the silence as they walked, after Angus had taken her twenty questions dig to heart and they'd talked most of the way here. About nothing particularly important, mostly about the Pilbara and the sights of Karijini Park—which Ivy had appreciated, still feeling a little raw from the night before.

There was just something about this man that had her revealing more than she ever intended.

In more ways than one, actually.

That thought made her smile, and she must have giggled, as Angus went still beside her.

'What's the joke?' he asked.

Ivy forced her lips into a horizontal line, and shook her head. 'I don't know what you're talking about.'

Which was completely the wrong thing to say, as now she'd intrigued him.

'Oh, really?' he said, 'Because—'

'Why don't you have a girlfriend?' Ivy blurted out, cutting him off.

Slightly horrified and with no clue where the question had come from, Ivy charged on ahead, although, given they were almost at the start of the walk down to Fortescue Falls, she really didn't have very far to go. At the lookout she pointed down into the abrupt one-hundred-metre-deep gash in the landscape.

'This is Dale Gorge,' she said. 'You can see the falls all the way down there.'

Angus, who had easily kept pace beside her, laughed. 'Yes, I got that.'

Ivy nodded. 'Of course. Right—so—this way!'

She knew he was still smiling, but decided not to pay any attention. Instead, she thought it was better to focus on her surroundings. It had been a couple of years since she'd been into Karijini. As she took in the vivid red of the ruthless, tiered red-brown cliffs and the rumbling sound of the falls beneath them, it seemed impossible she'd left it so long.

'I don't have a girlfriend because of my job,' Angus said.

Ivy tensed at the words, wanting to wish back her question. She had to walk slowly now. The path was narrow and twisting.

Angus was directly behind her, his boots crunching far more loudly than her sneakers.

'I'm not a fan of emotional farewells.'

She'd meant to remain silent, hopeful the subject would change, but once again she'd lost control of her mouth. 'But wouldn't that be worth it for the equally emotional welcome home?'

'I'm told I'm not much good at those either,' Angus said. Ivy sensed his shrug, even though she couldn't see him. 'Besides, that's only if I do come home.'

Ivy slipped on some gravel, and threw her hands out for balance. Instantly Angus's hands were on her, catching her at the waist before she could fall.

He quickly righted her, but slid his hands away just a little more slowly than was necessary.

'Thank you,' Ivy said softly, but was quick to start walking again.

Stupidly, she hadn't really put a lot of thought into Angus's career. She'd been caught up in the sexiness of it—the idea of a soldier: the uniform, the weapons, the courage. Not the reality, and certainly not the brutality of war and of death.

Her stomach had plummeted at his casual words: *only if I do come home*.

For their child, of course. She'd lost her father—not through death but through distance and lack of interest—and that had been difficult enough.

And maybe it had plummeted just a tiny bit for her.

'How do you do it?' she asked. 'How can you risk so much?'

They were about halfway into the gorge now, and the

colours of the rocks led the way—changing from orange to red to purple as they descended. To their left, the falls, which had seemed barely more than a trickle from a distance, now revealed their true size. A tourist, clambering along the adjacent rocks, gave some scale to the sprawling, towering year-round falls.

'Because I love it. The teamwork, the tactics, the challenge. It's what I've wanted to do since I was seventeen, and I'll do it for as long as I can.'

'But what about—?' Ivy began, but didn't really know how to continue.

'The bad stuff? You mean like death and destruction? Living under constant threat? Killing people?' He rattled off his terrible list roughly, and didn't wait for her to clarify. 'Of course that isn't fun. At times it's awful, actually. Indescribably awful. But then I get to come home.'

If he came home.

'And then a few months later, go and do it again.'

That was what Ivy couldn't wrap her head around. To survive war, and then risk it all again.

'Yeah,' he said. 'Sometimes—' he began, then stopped.

'Sometimes what?'

They were deep within the gorge now. Down here they walked amongst greenery and paperbarks—an incredible contrast to the parched landscape above.

'Sometimes I wonder if maybe it should be harder for me to go back.'

There was enough space for Angus to walk beside her, and she looked up at him.

'What do you mean?'

But he wasn't looking at her. Instead he lengthened his stride, then looked back over his shoulder. 'Come on, I'm keen to get to this Fern Pool you were talking about.'

He clearly wasn't going to answer her question, but still

Ivy very nearly repeated it. Besides, wasn't she just trying to get to know him better? Just as she was supposed to?

But it was something she'd glimpsed, however briefly, that meant she kept on walking in silence. For the first time since she'd met him he'd looked...

Ivy wouldn't have said *vulnerable*, because that wasn't even close to true. But something like that, something she'd never expected to see in Angus Barlow.

Angus had made it to the top of the falls, and he stood there, waiting for her.

He studied her as she approached, his gaze sweeping over her, the motion not all that dissimilar to the water as it rushed across the ancient, angular, straight-edged rocks, tracing the shape and lines of her.

But Ivy forgot to be annoyed or embarrassed by his attention, because she'd just worked it out—worked out what she'd seen.

Just for a moment, the shortest of moments, Angus had looked *exposed.*

Fortescue Falls was unusual. When Angus thought of waterfalls, he thought of a sheer pane of water, tumbling from a cliff. But here, the falls surged along a gradual series of steps and benches—like an elegantly curved stairway from amongst the trees down to the clear green pool below.

Ivy was playing tour guide, telling him that the waterfall flowed—miraculously—year round. She pointed out some of the vegetation and talked of local birds and bats. She was nervous, although Angus wasn't entirely sure why.

One moment she was so, so self-assured, the next self-conscious and talking too quickly, her gaze skittering away.

He didn't know what to make of her questioning his single status. Part of him liked it—liked that she'd wondered, liked that she'd been so appalled that she'd actually voiced the question. But another part of him—a big part—shied away from even such an oblique reference to a relationship between them. Ivy had been absolutely right to stop them both last night. Another night in bed together was not going to aid the relaxed, shared—and lawyer-free—parenting arrangement he kept telling Ivy he wanted.

Although of course it didn't mean he had to stop checking her out. She'd stepped away from him now to head down the track to Fern Pool, their true destination today. So of course he took the opportunity to have a good old look at her very nice view from behind.

It wasn't as if he hadn't noticed Ivy have a pretty thorough look at him at times.

Sex might be unwise. But looking didn't hurt anyone.

CHAPTER EIGHT

EXACTLY WHAT A terrible idea this had been only became clear to Ivy when she stepped onto the man-made wooden boardwalk that provided the only access to Fern Pool.

No one else was here, of course. Ivy had been here dozens of time with her family over the years, and *not once* had they had the pool to themselves. Even out here, more than a five-hour drive from the nearest major regional centre, tourists made sure they got to the Karijini. And they certainly made sure they got to Fern Pool.

Just not today.

Angus dumped his backpack onto the wooden boards, and Ivy looked determinedly across the crystal-clear water as he tugged off his T-shirt. Above them stretched a remarkable fig tree, and, of course, ferns were everywhere. It was lush, it was green, it was *wet*—everything that the desert-like Pilbara shouldn't be.

But it was also supposed to be full of tourists—a handful of lily-white British backpackers, a posse of raucous kids up here camping with their parents, or at least a pair of retired grey nomads.

Someone. *Anyone.*

Because without them, this place—this place with its mirror-flat water; its pair of tumbling waterfalls; its surrounding, towering layers and slabs of rock in reds and browns and purples was just…was just…

Undeniably, terribly and completely…romantic.

Dammit.

'You coming in?'

Angus stood directly in front of her, so of course she had to look at him. She made an attempt to stare only at his face, but almost immediately failed, her attention sliding rapidly downwards.

She'd felt that chest beneath her fingertips, felt it pressed hard against her.

But she hadn't had a chance to look at it—the moonlight in Bali had certainly not been as generous as the Karijini sun.

So she'd known he was broad, and hard, and ridiculously strong. But seeing him made it all new again. He was muscular, of course, but not in a stupid, body-builder way. There was still a leanness to him, a practicality—this man didn't just lift weights, he was fit, agile, supple.

He had a smattering of black hairs along his chest, but otherwise his skin was smooth. The occasional freckle dotted his lovely olive skin. His nipples were somehow darker than she expected. The ridges of his abdominal muscles deeper.

His board shorts sat low on his hips. He had that muscular V thing going on, and her eyes followed in the direction it was pointing...

Before she finally came to her senses and snapped her gaze back to his.

His grin was broad, and his eyes sparkled.

'So, Ivy—are you coming in?'

It was the same question, but also different. Was his voice lower? More intimate?

She took a deliberate step backwards, and promptly stepped onto his backpack, and the beach towels that Angus had pulled out for them.

It was the pool. The damned pool's fault for being so intimate and dreamily secluded.

Still grinning, Angus walked to the metal ladder that

provided access to the pool, although Ivy finally managed to drag her gaze away as he climbed in.

Instead she turned her back, as pointless as that was, to pull off her top and shorts. She liked that Angus had bothered to read the sign beside the pool, and he hadn't jumped in, as many others did. Ivy hadn't read it today, but she knew what the first line said: *Fern Pool is a special place.*

A place where you didn't make loud noises or jump off the waterfalls. Where you respected your surroundings and the traditional owners of the land.

It certainly shouldn't be a place where she ogled a half-naked man.

Her clothes neatly folded on top of Angus's backpack, Ivy rolled her shoulders back, and took a handful of long, deep breaths.

She told herself not to be self-conscious, although of course that was pointless. She could've been underwear-model thin and she *still* would've felt insecure around all of Angus's bronzed perfection.

And she certainly wasn't underwear-model thin. But she *was* in her favourite black and white striped bikini, and if she breathed in her stomach was almost flat.

Her hand rested on her still-normal-sized tummy.

She'd forgotten again.

Although this time, remembering that she was pregnant didn't trigger a spiralling panic, or make her want to squeeze her eyes shut and wish just about *everything* away if she could just find a way to fix what she'd done.

In fact, all it did was cause her to turn around, and to search for Angus in the water.

The pool wasn't large, but Ivy didn't have to search far anyway. His forearms rested on the edge of the boardwalk as he floated in the water, watching her.

'How long until the baby starts to move?' he asked.

'Ages,' Ivy said. 'Eighteen to twenty weeks, I think?'

Her lips quirked upwards. 'I thought you were full bottle on all this pregnancy stuff?'

He pushed away from the boardwalk, his eyes still on her. 'Haven't got to that chapter yet,' he said. He flicked his hand through the water, sending a light spray of water in her direction. 'I've noticed you're still not swimming.'

The drops of water that now decorated her feet were surprisingly cool, given the heat of the day. But then, down here, beneath the shade of the great fig, the light was diluted.

'Although I'm not really complaining,' Angus continued. He was treading water only metres from the ladder. Close enough that Ivy knew he was—and had been—checking her out.

She blushed, which was just about her default reaction to Angus it seemed, but also found herself smiling. Almost as if she was enjoying his attention.

Fern Pool romanticism *was* getting to her.

That was enough to get her into the water quick smart.

And it *was* cold. Cold enough that she gasped.

But just as she had as a kid, she immediately ducked beneath the water to soak her hair.

Better to get it over with quickly.

Ivy and Mila had always agreed on that approach. While April had swum around shrieking about not getting her hair wet *yet*, which had been pretty much an engraved invitation for her sisters to splash her with as much water as possible.

'What are you smiling about?' Angus asked, treading water beside her as she tucked her hair behind her ears.

'A nice memory,' she said, and then filled him in.

Angus rolled onto his back as she spoke, so he floated, staring up at the sky. 'It doesn't surprise me at all that you've always got straight to the point,' he said.

Except around Angus. Somehow, and sometimes, around

Angus, being direct seemed impossible. Her words escaped her. Her *brain* seemed to escape her.

'Do you have any brothers or sisters?' Ivy asked.

'No,' Angus said. 'Just Dad, and Mum, and me. We didn't really travel as a family all that much. You're lucky.'

Ivy laughed. 'We didn't always think that coming up here was all that great. But Mum was all for multitasking on a holiday—coming up here meant a business trip *and* a family getaway. Although my sisters and I did go to the US a few times to visit my dad.'

'The actor?'

'Yeah,' Ivy said, not surprised Angus knew that detail. Most people in Western Australia did—but then, a mining heiress didn't elope with a handsome, if small-time, Hollywood actor and have nobody notice. 'He left when I was pretty young, and we've never been close. He calls me on my birthday.'

She followed Angus's lead and stuck her legs and arms out so she could float on her back. Water lapped against her ears and she closed her eyes, enjoying the sensation of weightlessness.

'Are you close to your parents?' Ivy asked.

'Yes,' Angus said. 'And no. I mean—'

Ivy tilted her head so she could see him. He floated so close to her that if she reached out just a little bit further, their fingers would touch.

'I was very close to my father, but he…died. And my mother has early-onset dementia, which is pretty awful really.'

'Oh, that *is* awful,' Ivy said, jackknifing from her back to swim to him. 'I'm so sorry.'

He'd done the same thing, but he didn't wait for Ivy. Instead he swam away, in big, generous breast strokes, to the pair of tumbling waterfalls.

But he stopped just short of where the falls hit the pool,

and turned as he treaded water. 'I wish we had travelled together as a family more. But my dad worked too hard. Every weekend he was at the shop. He *had* to be at the shop—at the furniture shop we owned. Even when he didn't really need to be, he still thought he had to.'

Angus wasn't looking at her. His chin was tilted upwards, as if he was examining the thick, ropey branches of the fig tree that stretched towards the sky.

'My mum's like that,' Ivy said.

Now he looked at her. '*You're* like that,' he said.

'I am not!'

He simply raised an eyebrow.

Ivy opened her mouth to argue, but realised it was pointless. The fact was she wasn't very good at holidays. When she did go away, she kept one eye on her smartphone, and made damn sure she always had access to a Wi-Fi network.

But she'd hated how her mother had never truly been present on family holidays. She couldn't do that to her own child.

'I'd like to take our baby on holidays when he or she is older,' Angus said.

'Me too,' Ivy said. Then quickly added, 'Not with you, of course.'

'Of course,' he said, glancing at her with a smile. But there was a sadness to it, as if he was thinking of the family holidays he never had. Or the father he had lost.

'How old were you?' Ivy asked, 'I mean, when your dad died?'

'Seventeen,' he said. 'It was very sudden. I'd always thought I'd follow in his footsteps, continuing to run the family business or something. Although to be honest I hadn't worried too much about it. I was at an age where all I cared about was playing footy on the weekend. Or hanging out with my mates. I'd never had to deal with the future before.'

'So the army wasn't a lifelong dream?'

Another smile, but still without humour. 'No,' he said. 'Part of it was the physical aspect of the job. When dad died, I started to really get into my weights, and fitness. It was a distraction, I guess. A focus. As mum started to get unwell not long after. So the sense of achievement from lifting heavier weights or running further, or faster…it was… I don't know. Something. Something that wasn't thinking about what I'd lost, and what I was losing.' Angus wasn't looking at Ivy now, his gaze again focused somewhere in the giant fig's branches. 'But now I think it was a lot about the structure. The formality. With my dad gone and mum not really my mum any more—it was kind of a relief to have a schedule and orders to work to. Later, I fell in love with the job, with the mateship, the teamwork, the tactics. But early on the job was like an anchor for me, something I could rely on.'

'That's a heck of a lot for a young man to deal with,' Ivy said, her heart aching for a lost and grieving teenage Angus.

He nodded. 'Yeah,' he agreed. 'It was. Sometimes I wonder if—' But his words trailed off, and he turned back to the cascading water. 'Did you ever climb up behind the waterfall?'

Ivy blinked at the abrupt change of subject, but didn't push. Somehow she knew that Angus didn't share that story easily. If at all. 'All the time,' Ivy said, her tone consciously upbeat. 'It's slippery, though.'

He threw her an amused look, that sadness erased from his gaze.

'Oh, I'm sorry,' Ivy said, deadpan, as she swam up to the rocks. 'I should've realised you did slippery-rock training in the SAS.'

'Honey, you'd be amazed at what I can do,' he replied, and then, right on cue, slipped a little as he hoisted his legs onto the lowest, moss-slick rocks.

Ivy giggled, and Angus glared—but couldn't hide his grin.

The falls here were delicate in comparison to Fortescue, falling gently only about three metres from the protruding ledge of red rock above where they swam. Beyond the curtain of water, slabs of rock provided tiered seating of sorts, decorated with clumps of ferns.

It had been a while, but Ivy remembered which rocks provided the best grip, and it only took her a few seconds to clamber past Angus and to settle into her favourite spot—directly behind the waterfall, the tumbling water blurring and distorting the world around her into indistinct reds, blues and greens.

It didn't take long for Angus to join her, seated to her right. He stretched his longer legs out in front of him, just as Ivy had, although his toes also touched the falls. The sound of the water echoed back here, but it would still be easy to hold a conversation.

But they didn't say a word.

Instead, they both just sat silently together, not quite touching, looking through the waterfall.

At first, Ivy itched to speak. To say something. Anything.

But she couldn't.

Back here, on the other side of a blurry world, Ivy somehow knew that to talk would break this. Would break this moment, would destroy this unexpected sanctuary.

So while at first she'd wanted to shatter the silence, to pop the bubble of this special place, in the end she couldn't.

All she could do was sit here, and breathe in the scent of ferns and moss, and lick drops of water from her lips.

She'd propped her hands behind her, to balance herself on the rocks. Angus had done the same, but now he twisted slightly. Ivy turned to look at him, and his gaze locked with hers.

The light was different back here, and his eyes seemed different too. The flecks of green more emerald, the hazel base more gold.

As he looked at her he reached across his body, and skimmed the side of her thigh with his fingertips. His touch was impossibly, tinglingly light—and then it was gone.

There wasn't so much a question in his gaze. It was more he was simply waiting.

Because he knew, as she knew, where this was going to end.

But he needed to wait, because Ivy needed to wait.

Ivy needed to hold onto whatever tatty remnants of control she might still have when it came to Angus for as long as possible. He'd said, last night, that she couldn't control him.

Well, she couldn't control anything around Angus.

And now, just like last night, she really didn't want to. Despite everything.

She let go of a breath she'd been unaware she was holding, and something in Angus's expression shifted.

His gaze dropped to her lips, and his hand went back to her thigh.

But again, his touch was light.

Ivy didn't move. She couldn't really, without the possibility of sliding back into the pool. But again, she really didn't want to.

Her gaze followed the trail of his fingers.

Along the outside edge of her thigh, leaving a smattering of goose bumps.

Up, over her hip, and around the knot on the side of her bikini bottoms.

She was leaning back against her hands, so she was looking down her own body as his hand slid from her hip to lie, momentarily, flat against her belly.

Her gaze darted to his face, but his attention remained on her stomach, his expression unreadable.

Then he was on the move again, moving even more slowly now, tracing loops and circles along her ribs, beneath her breasts.

Her breath was coming more quickly now; she could see her chest rising up and down as warmth and need swirled within her.

Then, too quickly, his fingers moved up and over her bikini top, only brushing the swell of her breasts with the most frustratingly light movement.

But she couldn't protest, because words would end this.

Ivy didn't ever want this to end.

Everything she had was focused on his touch. Her eyes fluttered shut.

Over her collarbone. Across her shoulders. Up against the delicate, shivery cords of her neck.

Along her jaw, tilting her chin. Slowly, slowly, upwards.

His breath against her mouth. His hand sliding backwards and amongst her tangled hair.

Then, finally, his lips on her lips. His mouth on her mouth.

Cool, and firm, and tasting of the waterfall. Fresh, and perfect, and magical.

It was the most tantalising of any of their kisses. The most delicate, the most careful, the least carnal.

But it fitted this place.

And Ivy was lost amongst their kiss. She touched him only with her mouth but it was more than enough. She kissed him slowly, he kissed her leisurely, as if they had for ever.

Here, it felt as if they did.

Then a splash tore them apart.

A blokey laugh and then a yell: *'Cannonball!'*

Through the waterfall heads bobbed in the water, and then a shape flew through the air.

Another splash. More laughter.

They had company.

Angus was already on the move, and he turned to offer her his hand.

She shook her head, and smiled. 'No, I've got this.'

As she swam towards the boardwalk, Ivy knew that now was about when she should be feeling that familiar cloak of regret.

But she didn't.

She couldn't.

Angus did help her climb up the ladder, and gave her hand a little tug when she stood on the boardwalk, to pull her close so he could kiss her quickly—but firmly—on the lips.

Ivy knew what that was.

A promise.

And she shivered, despite the heat of the sun.

CHAPTER NINE

IVY FELL ASLEEP on the drive back to the homestead.

A combination of hours in the sun and early pregnancy fatigue.

And also, probably, that delicious lethargy from being so very thoroughly kissed.

She dreamed of that kiss, and of that place behind the waterfall.

When Angus shook her gently awake after he'd brought the car to a stop, it felt only natural to reach for him. To curl her hands behind his neck and to pull his lips down to hers.

But this was a totally different kiss from before.

This kiss wasn't slow, or gentle or restrained.

And neither was Angus.

There was a *click* as he released her seat belt, and then he was pulling her towards him, and then on top of him as he leant back in the driver's seat. Ivy smiled as she straddled him, rising up on her knees so she could reach his mouth.

His hands slid up to grip her butt, and then one slid upwards to reach beneath her top.

She still wore her bikini, dry now after the walk back from Fern Pool. It only took one tug on the string at the back to loosen the top half, and Angus just shoved the fabric away as he filled his hands with her breasts.

Ivy sighed into his mouth.

Their kiss before had been unforgettable, but this—this rawness, this lack of restraint—she *needed*.

And that need superseded any other emotion that did

its best to wave manically at Ivy from somewhere within her subconscious.

Because frankly Ivy knew that this was a bad idea.

The same way it had been a bad idea in Bali, and it had been a bad idea last night.

But that hadn't been enough to stop her then, and it certainly wasn't going to stop her now.

She needed this. Her structured, controlled, *planned* life had plummeted into a chaos that she had no idea how to fix. Maybe she couldn't fix it, and if she thought about that too long it terrified her.

But *this* felt good. *This,* at this moment, felt right.

Even if it wouldn't feel right tomorrow.

It didn't matter.

Angus's lips coasted along her jaw, pressing hard kisses along her neck.

'You good?' he said, deep and low, against her ear.

She nodded firmly *yes.* And as if that might not be clear enough, she said it aloud, too.

She felt his smile against her skin.

Ivy's hands had shoved his T-shirt up as much as was possible, her fingernails grazing his chest and those lovely muscles of his stomach, before she explored lower, sliding just beneath the top of his shorts.

Then Angus pushed her top up, and his mouth quickly covered her nipple, and Ivy went perfectly still.

His tongue was hot, gentle, rough, all at once. He took his time, licking, kissing—waiting for her reaction before doing again what made her sigh.

His big hands were flat on her back, holding her still. She sank down onto him as her head fell backwards, loving the feel of his hardness beneath her.

She impatiently shifted her hips, and Angus used his teeth, so, so gently, against her breast. *Later.*

But it already felt as if she'd been waiting far too long.

Since the waterfall. Since Bali.

Her hands had lain, useless and forgotten, on her lap, but now she put them to use, feeling for the snap closure on his shorts, as his head and shoulders blocked her view.

For a moment, she did go still, though. To watch him kiss her breasts. She had the same realisation every time she was close to him: he was *so* big, *so* broad, *so* overwhelming.

But right now, so careful. So focused.

On her.

It was a heady sensation. Sexy.

And she didn't just get to look at him, she got to feel him. Got to explore his strength, and experience how incredible all that controlled, amazing, coiled strength made her feel.

Finally she pulled the snap open, and it was easy to rip apart the Velcro fly on the board shorts.

He wore nothing beneath, and she shimmied backwards on his thighs so she could see what she'd just revealed.

Angus leaned back against the chair, and then, with a cheeky grin, reached down to adjust the chair so he reclined back further.

He looked so pleased with himself, Ivy grinned back, but then he reached for the button of her own shorts, and she formed her lips into a stern line.

Later.

She gripped his length in her hand, running her fingers from base to tip.

His breath had quickened, and he studied her from beneath half-lidded eyes.

She moved her hand again, enjoying the feel of him, the warmth and the sensation that he was growing even harder as she touched him.

'Ivy.'

The roughly spoken word dragged her attention back to his lips. She rose to her knees, desperately needing to kiss him again.

And when they did kiss, it was rough and messy and desperate.

Between them they unzipped her shorts, and somehow she managed to wiggle her way out of them, along with her bikini bottoms, twisting this way and that on Angus's lap.

'You're killing me here, Ivy.'

But finally she was free to straddle him again, and his hands cupped bare skin, gliding around to slide through her wetness, and to circle her where she needed it most.

She groaned, and kissed him again. Hard.

She reached for him, but then his lips were at her ear.

'I'm clean. There's been no one else since Bali.'

It shouldn't have been the perfect thing to say, but somehow it was. 'Me too,' she whispered.

And then she couldn't wait even a moment longer.

She wrapped her hand around him again, then slid, not slowly at all, downwards.

She sucked in a breath, the sensation of having him inside her, stretching her, filling her, almost *too* good.

But then she moved, and that was even better.

His fingers gripped her bottom, but she didn't need him to guide her. They fell instantly into the perfect rhythm, and his mouth found hers, kissing her again and again.

And the tension built inside her, growing and tightening low in her belly with every stroke and slide and sigh.

Then his clever fingers touched her where they were joined, and that was all it took to push her over an edge she'd felt she'd been teetering on for ever.

And fall she did, into wave after wave of sensation.

Then Angus was moving her hips harder, and faster, and the waves just kept on coming, overwhelming her in a way she'd never, ever experienced.

Then he was groaning into her ear, and finally, finally Ivy began to float back down to earth.

She lay there, sprawled on top of him, the four-wheel drive loud with their heavy, laboured breathing.

'Would it be wrong if I asked you to carry me inside again?' Ivy asked.

Her legs felt as substantial as fairy floss.

She sensed his smile, even though her face was pressed against his chest. 'No problem, just give me a minute. Right now, I just about need someone to carry me.'

And Ivy just smiled against his still-heated skin.

'So I have a theory,' Ivy said, a few hours later.

On Ivy's king-size bed, Angus rolled onto his side to face her. She stood in the en-suite doorway, wrapped in a pure white bathrobe, and with a towel twisted around her hair.

'Yeah?'

She nodded. 'A theory that makes this weekend okay.'

'This weekend is better than okay, Ivy.'

She narrowed her cool blue eyes. 'You know what I mean.'

She crossed the wide floorboards to perch primly on the edge of the bed. Angus sat up, the sheet puddled around his waist.

'Well, my theory is that you'd already seen me naked in Bali, so it isn't like this weekend makes any difference.'

'Because I would've been thinking of you naked whenever I saw you to pick up or drop off our kid, anyway.'

'No!' she said, swatting at his legs beneath the sheets. Then, 'Really?'

He shrugged. 'Of course. On the plus side, now I can imagine you in daylight.'

Ivy flopped onto her back on the bed and stared up at the ceiling. 'Oh, no.'

Angus grinned. 'Look, we both knew in Bali that we were just having fun. We both know now that we're just having fun. I'm sure we're both mature enough to behave like grown-ups in the future.'

'Except for the imagining me naked bit.'

'If it makes you feel better, I don't mind if you imagine me naked, too.'

Ivy tilted her head to glare at him.

'Do you want to hear my theory?' Angus said.

'Only if it doesn't involve nudity.'

'Done,' he said. He reached for the tie of Ivy's bathrobe, and tugged it open, just because he could. Ivy watched him, but didn't move, the hint of a smile on her lips. The terry towelling of the robe didn't move a lot, but it did reveal a lovely slither of skin. Not enough, though. 'Okay, so my theory is that this weekend is a great idea because clearly we needed more than Bali to get this thing out of our systems. If we *hadn't* slept together again, we would've had all this unresolved tension between us. This way we clear the air.'

'So having sex now will be good for our parenting in the future.'

'Exactly.'

'You should be in the Molyneux Mining marketing department,' Ivy commented.

'*You* shouldn't be wearing so many clothes.'

He moved so he was leaning across her, one hand on either side of her face.

'Well,' she said, very softly, 'technically I'm not wearing any clothes.'

Angus reached between them, pulling her robe completely open. He levered himself upwards, to survey what he'd revealed.

'You know what?' he said, after a very long while. 'I think you're right.'

He leant down, kissing her gently before pulling away to look at her again.

'Although, maybe I'll just check one more time.'

Ivy laughed, then tugged him down for another kiss.

Angus made breakfast again the next morning.

He'd woken beside Ivy after—as standard—another excellent night's sleep.

It had been a very long time since he'd last woken up in a woman's bed. A year, at least. Maybe two.

It was a slightly uncomfortable realisation.

He'd had girlfriends, of course. Nothing too long-term—a few months, maybe.

What he'd told Ivy yesterday had been partially true. He didn't like emotional farewells.

But not because *he* found them emotional.

It was stupid really, that the tears always surprised him. There he was, thinking everything was fine, that both he and the woman he was seeing were happy casually dating. And then the tears came. The earnest requests to keep in touch whenever he could.

Yet he never felt that way. He had no problem at all leaving. And if he was honest, it was more that he didn't make time—rather than that he forgot—to reply to emails or to video call home when he could.

So those farewells simply exposed a disconnect. Between the type of relationship he wanted—with no tears and no expectations—and the starkly, starkly different relationship his girlfriends had expected.

Eventually a pattern even he couldn't fail to miss had arisen amongst his ex-girlfriends' angry, parting words.

Thoughtless. Selfish. Cold. Distant.

And he'd realised, maybe around the time that Tom had left the regiment, that it was better if he didn't do relationships at all—even the most casual. So he might go out on the occasional date. But he'd never stay the night.

No expectations. No hurt feelings. No confusion.

He'd determined he simply wasn't wired for long-term relationships. For marriage. For commitment.

But everything had changed with Ivy's pregnancy. Now he, like it or not, had a permanent commitment—to his child. He'd have a child who might, once old enough, want to come and wave goodbye. Who would expect him to email or video call and would maybe even make one of those welcome home signs to hold on his return.

He hadn't planned this, but it was his new reality.

But what if he fell into his old habits? He'd been no good at maintaining a romantic relationship—what if the same applied to his child?

He remembered how much it had hurt when his dad had chosen hours in his office over his son. He'd adored his father, and deep down he'd known he was loved. But sometimes he had felt like an afterthought. Forgotten amongst the importance of work.

He didn't want to be that type of father. It was why he'd never intended to have children, to avoid the risk altogether.

So he needed to do everything he could to prevent that happening. To prevent his child being hurt.

It was why he was so persistent that he would be part of Ivy's life. They hadn't yet talked about how they would manage their co-parenting, how they would share custody—how they'd do anything. He knew, instinctively, that Ivy wasn't ready for that discussion yet.

But what he *did* know was that he needed to do this right.

Lawyers, obviously, wouldn't work. Neither would unresolved tension with Ivy.

'Morning.'

Ivy padded into the kitchen, rubbing her eyes. She wore a pale pink singlet and neat white underwear, and Angus honestly didn't think she'd ever looked more beautiful.

She hardly looked at him as she climbed onto the bar

stool. A hand reached up to pat ineffectually at her less than sleek hair.

'I couldn't bear to look in the mirror,' she said, looking at him with a half-lidded sleepy gaze. 'But I still suspect I should apologise for the state of my hair.'

No, last night she'd been a bit too distracted after her shower to think about drying it.

'You look stunning,' he said, meaning it.

She stuck out her tongue. 'Ha-ha.' Then she grinned. 'But I forgive you, because you've made me breakfast again.'

'Pancakes, bacon, bananas and maple syrup,' he said.

'Bacon?'

'It's a taste sensation,' he said. 'Trust me.'

She raised a sceptical eyebrow, but tucked into her breakfast, none the less.

Later, she helped him load the dishwasher.

'I wouldn't have picked you as a cook,' she said.

'Don't get too excited—breakfast is my speciality.' He could've left it at that, but then found himself still talking. 'My mum was an incredible cook. I guess I picked up a few things from her. I do a mean lasagne.'

'I'd love to try it one—' Ivy began, then stopped abruptly.

She took an already clean plate to the stainless-steel bin, and scraped at it with a knife to remove non-existent scraps.

I'd love to try it one day.

The atmosphere in the kitchen had shifted.

Before it had been all light, and flirtatious, with everything they said and did touched by the afterglow of the night they'd shared.

But with that one short sentence, this wasn't the casual, one-off weekend they'd agreed to last night.

Sun still streamed through the huge sliding doors, but now it seemed *too* bright. As if it were shining a light on all that was wrong with this image, rather than all that was superficially right.

He should have returned to his own bed last night.

Maybe it was just a slip of the tongue. Maybe Ivy wanted nothing more, either.

But it had been unwise to persist with this faux cosiness, this illusion of a sexy weekend away between a loved-up couple—complete with a home-cooked breakfast.

He didn't want this.

He didn't want any of this.

But more importantly, he wasn't capable of it, either.

CHAPTER TEN

THE DRIVE TO Paraburdoo could only be described as awkward.

As was the flight home.

They spoke, but it was terribly, terribly polite.

Everything had changed so quickly. One moment all was well, and Angus had been all warm and sexy; the next it was clear—*so clear*—that it was over.

But what was *it*?

It was dangerous. As dangerous as how she'd felt when she'd woken to the smell of pancakes, or when Angus had kept touching her so subtly as they'd cleaned the kitchen. A hand on her hip, here. A deliberate brush of her fingers, there.

So, so dangerous.

She should be grateful she'd made that silly comment. And logically, she was.

She'd known that it would end, and soon. Was it wrong that she'd hoped it to last even a few hours longer? Could it really hurt if they'd pretended until they arrived back in Perth?

Or at least until they'd left the homestead?

Well, of course it could. Because what would it have achieved? Really?

A few more kisses. Maybe more, if they'd been quick. *No. Stop it.*

Ivy had her hands rested neatly on her lap as she sat in the back seat of her car. It took everything she had not to twist them into knots. Because Angus sat beside her.

That had been another brilliantly awkward conversation:

'I'll get a taxi home.'

'Don't be stupid. I insist.'

'Ivy—'

'Please just let me drive you home.'

And however she'd said that last bit had finally convinced him. That bothered her, too.

What had she revealed for him suddenly to agree? Why had she even cared?

Why couldn't he have just signed the bloody contract?

Why? Why? Why?

The car rolled to a stop on a quiet, tree-lined street in Swanbourne. Ivy didn't know what she'd expected, but the lovely federation cottage with its neat box hedges and generous sprays of lavender was definitely not it.

'It was my mum's,' Angus said, reading her mind. 'But I like it.'

She liked that he did, not that it mattered.

'I'd imagined something more...macho,' she said.

'And what does that mean?'

Something modern and concrete and angular?

No. That didn't fit Angus.

'I don't know,' she said. 'Maybe a log hut where you drag the food you've hunted with your bare hands?'

Angus barked a surprised laugh, the sharp sound unexpected amongst the still-simmering tension. 'You're unique, Ivy,' he said.

She liked that he'd said that too.

He grabbed his backpack, and climbed out of the car.

He didn't say goodbye. He didn't look back, either; he just walked up the recycled brick path to his front door.

'We going straight to your place, Ms Molyneux?' her driver asked, looking in his rear-view mirror.

Ivy realised she was staring at the now-closed cottage door.

She gave her head a little shake.

'Yes,' she said. 'Thank you.'

The weekend was over.

'Ivy? Are you listening?'

Ivy blinked. She was at April's place, a lovely house perched on the beach in North Cottesloe. She held a mug of hot chocolate in her hands, and she'd been watching April as she'd talked, but, as hard as she tried, she hadn't really been listening.

It was three days since she'd arrived back from Bullah Bullah Downs, and yet Angus still crowded her thoughts.

She tried to tell herself that was normal; after all, she'd never had such a casual—uh—*relationship* before, so it probably made sense that the experience would linger.

It was just that the lingering had been at *the* most inappropriate times. Like during an important conference call today when she'd completely lost her train of thought, or now—when clearly April had just told her something important.

'I'm sorry. Something's on my mind.'

'I know, I know,' April said, with the air of the long suffering, '*work.*'

Ivy opened her mouth to correct her sister, but then snapped it shut. No. It was impossible to tell April only part of the story, and she still wasn't ready.

'Well,' April said, dragging out the word theatrically, 'I know it's a bit earlier than I've always said, but Evan and I have decided to try for a baby!'

Ivy went completely still.

April was beaming. 'I know it's kind of weird to tell you—I mean, basically I'm telling you that Evan and I are having lots of unprotected sex—but, you know, I just *had* to tell somebody.'

It took some effort, but Ivy arranged her lips into a smile. 'That's brilliant, April, how exciting.'

April tilted her head, studying Ivy. 'You okay?'

Ivy nodded vigorously. 'I'm fine. And I'm *thrilled* for you.'

And she was. Just the secret that she was keeping from everyone now felt a million times larger.

'I'm going to tell Mila too. *Not* Mum though.' Her sister paused. 'I'd rather keep it a big surprise for her and tell her when we fall pregnant. She'll be over the moon!'

'You think?' Ivy asked, surprised. 'She wasn't all that maternal with us.'

They'd had a team of wonderful nannies to look after them while their mother worked her incredibly long hours. She still worked those hours, now.

'Of course. Who wouldn't want to be a grandmother?'

'I suppose,' Ivy said, but didn't really agree.

But then, her relationship with her mother had always been different from that of Mila and April. Her mother had always been tougher on her, always held her to a higher standard of achievement, always pushed her harder. Because—her mother said—*you're just like me.*

Now would be the perfect time to tell April of her pregnancy.

Right *now.*

Because now she didn't just feel as if she were omitting something, she felt as if she was outright lying.

But April would shriek with excitement and ask a million questions and be all joyful and just plain *happy*, and she wouldn't understand when Ivy tried to explain why she was so damn terrified about it all. So. Now wasn't the right time.

But she did have to tell her. And Mila, and her mother.

Soon. Very soon, because she couldn't keep hoping she'd miraculously come up with a better plan.

It wasn't going to happen.

And as nice as it would be to tell only April and Mila, and to bask in their excitement before they started to connect the dots and work out what it actually meant for Molyneux Mining, the better way was to tell them all together.

Because her mother would connect the dots immediately. She'd leap right to the point, because that was what she did. As in business, it would be better that way.

April had left the room, and came back now with a small pile of pregnancy magazines, which she placed carefully on the coffee table in front of Ivy.

'Look, I know this is totally jumping the gun, but honestly, I don't know *anything*, and none of my friends have had kids yet, and...'

Yes. She'd tell them all at dinner on Sunday.

That evening, Angus pushed the buzzer on the stainless-steel panel bolted to Ivy's limestone fence, and waited.

After a minute, Ivy's voice came through the speaker. 'Yes?'

'It's Angus,' he said.

He'd then fully expected to have to explain why he was here, but instead the gate immediately began to open.

Surprised, he climbed back into his car, and drove up the neat driveway.

Ivy stood with her arms folded at the base of the steps that led to her front door, dressed in jeans and a loose T-shirt, waiting for him.

He jumped out of his car, and slammed the door behind him. 'I expected that to be more difficult.'

'I expect that people call before visiting,' Ivy said, one eyebrow raised. Her hair was loose, and a few tendrils blew across her cheeks in the evening breeze.

He shrugged. 'I was concerned that warning you may have resulted in another contract on arrival.'

'I let you in because I didn't want you to pull another stunt like at the airport.'

Angus grinned. 'I like that. Now I'm a stuntman, *and* a soldier.'

Ivy rolled her eyes, but his comment had the desired effect as she couldn't hide a subtle smile. 'I suppose you want to come in?'

'Up to you,' he said. 'I'm mainly here for a delivery.'

He held out a small brown paper bag.

Now he'd intrigued her. 'For me?'

'Don't get too excited.'

She took the bag, and he could see her warring with her inherent politeness.

'It's dark,' she said, eventually. 'Come inside, I'll open it in there.'

He followed her into the house. They walked past a broad, curving staircase and elaborate leadlight doors to the open-plan kitchen and living area.

While the kitchen was modern, the house seemed to have retained most of its original features—with detailed ceiling mouldings, a high plate rail on the walls and wide polished jarrah floorboards. The furniture was a mix of old and new, and it felt as if Ivy had decorated it, rather than some fancy interior designer.

He liked it, and he told her so.

Ivy smiled. 'Thanks. I used to walk past this house on the way to school. I always wanted to live here when I was a kid. I thought it was magical with all its arches and curves, and the Juliet balcony upstairs. My mum bought it for me after...' Her words trailed off as she walked over to the fridge. 'Would you like a drink?'

'That's quite a gift.'

'Well,' Ivy said, 'at the time my mum wanted to make quite the gesture.'

'About what?'

Ivy held open the fridge door and pointed at the shelves. 'Juice? Wine? Beer? Water?'

'Beer,' he said. He hadn't planned to stay, but now he couldn't remember why.

He watched her as she carried the beer to the bench, and then located a bottle opener in her cutlery draw.

Her jeans were faded and loose, as if they were her old favourites—and he imagined her taking off her tailored work clothes to slide into them.

Which wasn't the greatest idea.

He immediately wondered if she'd worn the same style of underwear today as she'd worn in the Pilbara: plain and simple but incredibly—incredibly—sexy. Or if she'd worn a skirt to work today like the one she'd worn when they'd had lunch. Prim, and fitted and—yep—incredibly sexy as well.

'Let's just say,' Ivy said, 'that my mother was keen to end what she considered my *rebellious* phase.'

It took him a moment to remember what they'd been talking about.

'Aren't you going to ask me when *I* was ever rebellious?' she prompted.

He shook his head. 'It doesn't surprise me at all.'

Ivy pushed the now-opened bottle across the kitchen bench towards him. She leant one hip against the granite, a glass of juice in her hand.

'Really?' she said, and seemed pleased. 'I don't think anyone has ever thought me capable of being a rebel.'

'But you just said you were.'

This wasn't making a lot of sense.

Her gaze darted downwards, as if she now found her juice endlessly fascinating. 'I wasn't, not really.'

'Just enough for your mum to buy you a house so you'd stop being one.'

'No, it wasn't like that,' Ivy said to the flecks of stone in the bench top. 'I mean, yes, I did say that, but...' Then she looked up and caught Angus's gaze. 'Really, it doesn't matter, does it? My mum bought me a house, which probably fits every spoilt-little-rich-girl stereotype ever, and that's the end of it.'

She'd left the bag he'd handed her on the corner of the bench, near where Angus stood, and now she strode over to pick it up, clearly hoping to change the subject.

Her movements were rushed and awkward, and it took some effort for Angus not to reach out for her—but to do what, he wasn't sure.

'Ivy, you go after what you want, and what you think is right,' Angus said, deciding if he couldn't reassure with his touch, he'd try something else. 'I might not always agree with you, but I can still respect your drive, your focus. So yes, if what you wanted wasn't the "right" thing to do, I have no trouble imagining you rebelling.'

Ivy studied him for a moment, with wariness in her eyes—as if waiting for a punchline.

But after a while, her lips curved into half a smile. 'Thank you,' she said. 'That was a nice thing to say.'

'And for what it's worth,' he added, 'I don't think anything about you is stereotypical. Of anything, or anyone.'

Her smile broadened. 'Are you saying I'm a bit weird?'

He grinned, too. 'You know I'm not.'

Her gaze dropped again.

He tapped at the bag she was still holding. 'Can you hurry up and have a look?'

When she looked up her gaze was teasing again. 'Goodness, you're pushy!'

'You're surprised?'

Then she laughed, and it was as if all that awkwardness—and whatever it was she'd almost told him—had never happened.

She dumped the contents of the bag onto the bench.

A couple of thick, glossy booklets; an application form; and a few other bits and pieces he'd printed off the Internet.

'A learner's permit application?' Ivy asked, picking up the offending piece of paper as if it had a disease. 'Why would you think I'd want this?'

'Because I think it's crazy that a woman your age, in a city like Perth with less than stellar public transport, *doesn't* have a licence.'

Ivy shrugged. 'I'm not going to get a licence just to make you feel better.'

'No, although I'm surprised you'd be comfortable being the only mum in your mothers' group being dropped off with bub in a limo. Now, *then* you'd be fitting every spoilt-little-rich-girl stereotype in the book.'

Her eyes narrowed. 'Did you come across mothers' groups in all your researching?'

No, actually. Tom had told him, years ago, after a 'swarm of babies' had descended on his home a few months after he'd had his first.

'I can come up with other similarly awkward scenarios, especially as our baby grows up. I don't know about you, but I would've hated being dropped off at footy training in the family Rolls Royce with a driver in a silly hat in the front seat.'

'I don't own a Rolls, or a silly hat for my driver to wear,' Ivy said, but the bite had gone from her words.

'I've hit a nerve?'

Ivy ran her hands through her hair, absently piling it up on top of her head before letting it tumble back down to her shoulders. 'You can be very annoying, you know that?' she said, then sighed. 'I used to get crap at school because I had a driver drop me off, not my mum. Everyone thought I was a snob—which is saying something given I went to a very posh school. My sisters were good at dealing with that sort of teasing, but I was just rubbish at it. I tend to think of clever things to say half an hour after it would've been useful.' She looked down at her tummy. 'What if this little bub takes after me in that way, and not you?'

'True,' he said, with a completely straight face, 'that would be tragic.'

Ivy reached out to gently shove him on the shoulder. 'Ha-ha. Let me guess—you were the most popular boy in school?'

'Close,' he said. 'Maybe third most popular is more accurate.'

He was only partly teasing. School had been a lot of fun for him—until his father's sudden death had ripped it all away.

Ivy was looking at him curiously. 'You okay?'

Angus deliberately smiled, annoyed that he'd revealed something in his expression.

'Of course. So—you're going to get your licence, then?'

Slowly, Ivy nodded. 'Yeah,' she said. 'It would seem so.'

'Great!' he said, with a little more enthusiasm than was necessary. 'I'll come over on Sunday for your first lesson.'

'Pardon me?'

Angus took a long sip of his beer. 'I'll teach you,' he said. 'We still have a lot to work out before the baby arrives—and we'll need to come to some sort of parenting arrangement so access, financial issues and so on are clear between us. And I still think it's important we continue to get to know each other better.' He paused, then added, 'Clothed.'

As he'd intended, Ivy blushed a deep scarlet.

'Are you sure that's the best idea?' she asked. 'We can have those discussions in a meeting room at the Molyneux Tower. Or my lawyer's office. Keep it more formal. And surely they can wait a few months, anyway?'

'I can't see any benefit in a delay,' Angus said. 'Especially as I could be deployed at any time once I return to work.' He raised an eyebrow. 'But what are you worried about? Am I that irresistible?'

Ivy glared at him. 'I know that *I'm* clear that we can't... um—'

'Have sex?' he prompted helpfully.

'Yes,' she said. 'We can't do that again. It's too complicated.'

'Agreed,' he said.

But still it took some effort to leave his half-drunk beer with a comment that he needed to drive home, and to make his exit only a few minutes later.

It would've been far too easy to stay.

CHAPTER ELEVEN

'YOU BOUGHT A new car?'

Angus stood in front of Ivy on her driveway, dressed in faded jeans and a T-shirt, squinting—somehow attractively—just a little in the bright early afternoon sun.

Ivy smiled, running a hand along the neat Volkswagen hatchback's glossy silver hood. 'Yes. I thought it was better to learn in a smaller car, rather than your giant four-wheel drive. Also, apparently it's better to learn to drive a manual.'

'So you bought a new car,' Angus repeated, shaking his head.

She shrugged. 'I don't think it's that big a deal.'

Ivy had embraced this 'learn to drive' project a little more zealously than was necessary, she knew. She'd read the books Angus had left her, done a couple of online mock learner's quizzes, then gone in to sit her learner's test at the local licensing centre during her lunch break the very next day.

Buying the car had been surprisingly fun. She'd never really given any car a second thought, but suddenly she was reading motoring reviews, going out for test drives with her assistant, and picking out her favourite colour.

She was enjoying the distraction; it meant she had something else to think about whenever her day wasn't wall-to-wall Molyneux Mining that wasn't her pregnancy, or Angus.

And cars were a lot less scary to think about than what on earth she was going to tell her mother and sisters that night at dinner.

Or so she'd thought.

It was one thing to agree with Angus's irritatingly accurate logic and to get her learner's permit. But quite another to actually, physically drive.

Angus theatrically opened the driver's door for her. 'After you, m'lady.'

With a deep breath, Ivy slid into her seat. Once seated and strapped in, she focused on her breathing.

One in, two out, three in, four out, five in, six out...

It was the first time in weeks she'd counted anything, although it wasn't all that surprising.

The breathing had helped when she'd first got in a car again when she was nineteen. So had the counting.

In fact, that was when the counting had started. All those years ago, as she shook with nerves in the passenger seat of her mother's car.

Seven in, eight out, nine in...

Angus was explaining something. 'So from left to right it goes clutch, brake, accelerator,' Angus said, pointing at the pedals at her feet. 'Remember it's just ABC, in reverse.'

Ivy nodded, although it was a bit difficult to focus on what he was saying beyond her mental counting.

He then talked her through how to use her mirrors, and Ivy managed to follow his instructions well enough to adjust both the rear-view and side mirrors sufficiently.

Then she fussed around quite a bit adjusting her seat.

Too far forwards. Too far back. Too far forwards again.

Seat-back was too upright. Too reclined.

Then she found she could lift the seat up and down. So she did that a bit too, the little motor whirring away as she pushed the up and down buttons.

But eventually she'd adjusted as much as was possible, so had to sit still.

'Don't be nervous,' Angus said. 'You'll be fine.'

It was lucky Ivy was wearing sunglasses, because otherwise Angus wouldn't be so sure. She'd tried this once before, years ago.

She remembered how she'd looked then, in that mirror behind the sun visor. She'd flipped it down and stared into her own eyes as she'd given herself a little lecture:

You can do this, Ivy. Everyone learns how to drive. Don't be so pathetic.

It hadn't worked then, but surely now—twelve years later—she would've got over it all?

Surely?

'Ivy?' Angus asked gently. 'Can you start the car? Foot on clutch, gear in first. The handbrake is still on, so we won't go anywhere.'

Ivy guessed he'd given her these instructions more than once, but they might as well have been gobbledegook.

Regardless, she put her left hand on the gear stick, and shoved her left foot down hard on the clutch. With a wiggle that was probably too rough, she put the car into first gear.

There.

A ghost of a smile curved her lips. *Maybe she would do it this time?*

Hand back on the wheel, she reached with her right hand for the keys.

All she had to do was twist the key forward and…

She couldn't do it.

She snatched her hand away—why she wasn't sure— and the key dropped to the ground, landing with a thud on the soft carpeted floor.

'Ivy?'

But she didn't wait; instead Ivy threw open her door and leapt from the car, running up her front steps two at a time.

At her door she realised she'd left her handbag—and house keys—in the back seat of her new car.

When she pivoted back to the car, Angus was right

there—only a metre or two away. He'd taken his sunglasses off, and concern was obvious in his gaze.

Ivy kept hers on, despite the shade of the veranda.

'You're not just nervous,' Angus said.

'No,' she said.

'And the reason you don't have a licence is nothing to do with being a spoilt little rich girl who couldn't be bothered.'

'No.'

'Can you tell me the real reason?'

No.

'I was in a car accident when I was nineteen.'

That was more than she'd told anyone, ever. More than anyone else, but her mother, knew.

Oddly, even though she hadn't meant to say the words, it felt good to say them.

'Were you hurt?'

Ivy shook her head. She didn't want to say this bit. This bit wouldn't feel good to say.

'A few bruises, a big one from the seat belt,' she said. 'But nothing, not really.'

She'd often felt it would've been better if she had been injured. A gash to her face that everyone noticed. A scar on her skin, and not just on her insides.

'You were the passenger?'

Angus had stepped closer. His hand moved, and for a second Ivy thought he was reaching for her, but then the moment was gone.

'My boyfriend was driving us home. He'd taken me to this club, a pretty seedy private one, upstairs somewhere in Northbridge. He'd been drinking, a lot, but he insisted on driving home.' Now she'd started talking, the words wouldn't stop. 'I'd only been seeing him for a few weeks. He was really tall, with overlong brown hair and an eyebrow ring. He had tattoo sleeves up both arms, but one was only half inked in. I thought it *so* cool. I thought he was *so* cool. He wasn't like any guy I'd met before. He wasn't rich. He wasn't poor, either, but I kind of pretended he was—like he was the kid from the wrong side of the tracks and I was the sweet rich girl he was going to corrupt.'

'He was your rebellious phase,' Angus said.

'Oh, yes,' Ivy said. 'I wanted to rebel so badly that I grabbed the first vaguely disreputable guy I could find and held on tight. We barely knew each other, really. All we did was go out drinking and clubbing. But I thought I was in love, you know? I'd spent my whole life being the perfect firstborn daughter, and now I wasn't. Although I wasn't all that brave. I told my family I was with girlfriends. So I was kind of rebelling on the sly.'

Ivy smiled without humour. She knew she was saying too much, and all jumbled in the incorrect order—but she couldn't stop.

'So Toby drove me home. I knew he'd had too much to drink, and I told him I'd call one of the family drivers to come pick us up. Or I'd pay for a taxi. And honestly, he looked at me like I'd just suggested we take ballroom-dancing classes.' She shook her head. 'I knew he shouldn't drive. I mean, I didn't even have a *sip* of alcohol until I turned eighteen. I'm that person. I'm the annoyingly sensible one. But that night I decided I wasn't. That I was cool and relaxed. But I wasn't. I couldn't relax. I basically held onto my seat for dear life, and Toby noticed, and got angry, and told me I had to trust him.' Ivy kept entwining and untwining her fingers, again and again. 'And he drove faster. And faster. And I told him not to, at first I tried to sound relaxed but then I was literally screaming at him as he thundered down the street.' A long pause. 'Then he lost control, hit a tree, and was killed instantly.'

The simple words, in a way, reflected that night. In the end, it was so simple. One moment Toby was there, beside her: loud and arrogant and drunk. Then—gone. Just like that.

'What an idiot,' Angus said.

'He paid a high price for his mistake,' Ivy pointed out.

'But he almost took you with him.'

Ivy couldn't argue with that. 'The whole driver's side of the car caved in. I had to be cut out of the wreckage, but I was okay. Totally okay. I walked away.'

That night was still mostly a blur. She'd had a few drinks herself, although she'd been far from drunk.

Her memories were more little snapshots from the night: Toby's smile when she'd walked into the bar and he'd checked out her too-short skirt; putting her mobile phone back into her bag, without making that call for a driver; the click of her seat belt when she strapped herself in; Toby's frenzied, ugly, manic expression when she'd pleaded with him to slow down, to stop, to let her out...

Then the impossible arrangement of Toby's seat and the steering wheel after impact. The feel of his pulseless wrist beneath her fingertips.

Ivy hadn't realised she'd closed her eyes until she felt her sunglasses being lifted from her face.

She blinked up at Angus. He was very close, but not touching her.

'But you weren't okay,' Angus said. 'No one is okay after something like that.'

Ivy bit her lip, and ignored him. 'When the police arrived, they found drugs in the car. I was so stupid and naïve I'd had no idea. I didn't even know what drugs they were. I still don't. And the worst bit is that even if I had known, I was so caught up in Toby and his tattoos and being an edgier version of myself it probably would've only added to Toby's mystique. The police questioned me at the hospital, but then my mum arrived, and it all went away.'

'What does that mean?' he asked. He still stood close. Too close, probably, but Ivy didn't mind. It helped, actually.

'It means what I said. My mum made it all go away. I don't know what she did. I didn't ask. Maybe I wouldn't have been in trouble, anyway? Who knows? All I know is that when I went home, my sisters didn't know I'd been in a car accident. When I read about the crash in the papers the next day, there was no mention of me. It's like I was erased from the whole incident.' She paused, thinking. 'It wouldn't be all that hard. I know the right people to call, now, should I want a story pulled. For Molyneux Mining, it's important to have a close relationship with the media. Bad publicity can be so damaging.'

'But what about the damage to a teenager?' Angus asked, his words harsh.

Ivy had been staring at the print on the front of his T-shirt, but now her gaze shot up to meet with his. 'I would've been a lot more damaged if the story had got out,' she said. 'It would've followed me for ever. It was difficult at the time, but I'm grateful for what my mum did. It turned me around, set me back on track.'

'On track to take over Molyneux Mining next year.'

Ivy nodded sharply. 'Yes.'

'And you never made another mistake again.'

'Yes,' Ivy said, automatically. 'I mean, no, of course I've made mistakes. I make mistakes all the time.'

'But nothing big. Nothing that would ever have anyone question Ivy Molyneux's competence, or business sense, or suitability to take over the company.'

'No one would *dare* do that,' Ivy said, getting annoyed. 'I would never do *anything* to jeopardise Molyneux Mining. I learnt my lesson.'

Angus studied her, his gaze tracing her eyes, nose and lips, then returning to meet her gaze. 'I get it now,' he said.

'The marriage proposal, the contract. Your rabid need to fix everything, to control everything.'

Ivy bristled, but he didn't let her speak.

'It's because you actually think it's possible, don't you? That you can do what your mother did all those years ago, and sweep it up—make everything uncomfortable, messy and awkward just disappear. Just go away without any consequences.'

'It is possible,' Ivy said, stubborn enough to argue. 'And there are *always* consequences. Like how I can't drive.'

That poor attempt at a joke received only a look of derision.

'It's about minimising damage,' she continued. 'About controlling the...'

But she heard what she was saying and knew she was going around in circles.

Suddenly she *was* standing too close to Angus. She stepped around him, intended to go and get her bag out of the car. There wasn't going to be a driving lesson today.

She should get inside. Get some work done.

But Angus grabbed her hand.

Ivy spun around to face him, snatching her hand away. 'But *you* won't go away, will you?' she said. 'No matter how I ask you, or what I say, or what I offer...'

'No,' he said.

One simple word, but it made her want to scream.

But scream at what?

That, as he'd told her before, she couldn't control him?

Or scream at the fact that she didn't really want him to go away at all?

Ivy's shoulders slumped.

She couldn't pretend any more. She wasn't miraculously going to come up with a plan. She wasn't going to fix this. This wasn't going to go away.

'I'm telling my family tonight,' she said, very quietly.

'I'll come with you.'

'I didn't ask you to come,' she said.

'You never would,' he said, stepping closer to her again. 'But I'd like to be there. Maybe it would help.'

Ivy was absolutely sure it wouldn't. He would only complicate the most complicated of situations.

And yet…

'Okay,' she said.

She'd told herself she didn't want him to come, but couldn't quite make herself believe it.

He took another step closer, and she tilted her chin upwards. Then, before she really knew what was happening, he kissed her.

A soft kiss, a gentle kiss.

'It'll be okay,' he said, against her lips.

She stood stock-still as he skirted around her and walked to his car.

'What time should I pick you up?' he asked.

'Six-thirty,' she said.

And then he was gone.

Of course, it wasn't a surprise that Ivy's mother lived in a palatial mansion. Angus had expected nothing less.

The dining room was very grand. The table was long enough to allow space for two chandeliers above it, and the table was set like something from a magazine, with white flowers everywhere.

Ivy's sisters sat at the table. The pair had been chattering loudly as they'd walked into the room, but when they saw him they instantly fell silent.

Through another door, Ivy's mother entered the room with a bottle of champagne.

'Oh,' she said, her gaze flicking over him. 'I'd better get another table setting.'

Then she turned on her heel, and walked out.

Ivy was incredibly tense beside him. Very, very softly, she was counting under her breath.

His instinct was to put his arm around her, but he knew that wouldn't help.

Although, in fact, his true instinct was not to be here at all.

He hadn't done this before—this 'meeting the family' thing. So far, he wasn't much of a fan.

'Thirty-seven...thirty-eight...'

He reached out and wrapped his hand around Ivy's.

Maybe it wouldn't help, but maybe it would.

Ivy glanced up at him, and attempted a smile.

There was a clink and clatter at the table as Ivy's mum returned and set a place for Angus.

She walked to him, holding out her hand. 'I'm Irene.'

He needed to drop Ivy's hand to shake Irene's, and instantly Ivy stepped away. She rushed to the table, and dropped into her seat as if they'd been playing musical chairs.

'Angus Barlow,' he said.

Irene's handshake was firm, but that was no surprise. She studied him with care, distrust flickering in her blue eyes.

This also was no surprise. He'd bet his house that Ivy hadn't brought another man to Sunday dinner before.

A minute later they were all seated. Irene's personal chef came out to talk them through the upcoming courses, and shortly afterwards their entrées arrived. A tiny stack of vegetables and salmon, with a sauce smeared theatrically across the plate.

April and Mila remained silent, seated across from them, as if waiting for Ivy to speak. They snuck curious glances in his direction, and the tiniest of encouraging smiles.

Irene sat at the head of the table, to Angus's right. Her lips were formed into a perfectly flat line.

But she was waiting, too.

No one touched their cutlery. No one picked up their glass of champagne.

And the tension just continued, and continued to build.

Ivy took a long, deep breath.

Then she shifted in her chair so that she faced her mother.

Another long, deep breath.

'I'm pregnant,' she said.

Silence.

'I'm the father,' Angus said, because he couldn't let Ivy do this alone.

But Irene didn't pay any attention to him. Instead she surged from her seat and went to one of the room's huge windows, staring out into the night.

'Oh, my *God*!' April shrieked, clapping her hands together. 'Ivy! That's amazing! Congratulations!'

Ivy picked up her water glass, then put it back down again, untouched.

Mila's reaction was more subdued. Her gaze flicked between Angus and Ivy. 'Was this planned?'

Ivy shook her head, but didn't seem capable of speech.

'No,' Angus said, unnecessarily, but needing to say something.

'You kept *this* on the down low, Ivy,' April said, indicating the two of them—and seemingly oblivious to Ivy's discomfort. 'When did you start going out?' She paused, then laughed. 'Goodness, I was so distracted at the wedding I didn't notice *anything* between you. Can you believe it?'

April turned to her younger sister, but Mila was watching Ivy.

'We're not—' Ivy began.

'Going to bore you all with how we met,' Angus finished for her.

Ivy's eyes widened in surprise, but she didn't correct him.

'What will you do next year?' Mila asked, and at her question Irene turned from the window, crossing her arms in front of her chest.

'Yes,' the older woman said, her gaze steely. 'What are we going to do?'

Not 'you', but 'we'.

'Well,' Ivy said, 'around about July, *I'll* be having a baby.'

There. There was a bit of the bite and sass he was used to.

'Don't be facetious, Ivy,' Irene said. 'I think you understand what is at stake here.'

'Of course I understand what's at stake here, Mum,' Ivy said. She pushed back her chair, and stood up, gripping the edge of the table. 'I'd like to negotiate a period of maternity leave, and a delay to me taking over your position. I do apologise for that, but it's unavoidable.'

'Unavoidable?' Irene zeroed in on Angus now. 'I have no idea who you are, but I'm sure you've heard of condoms?'

April and Mila both looked mildly scandalised that their mother had said *condoms*.

Angus leant back in his chair, deliberately relaxing his body, knowing that would infuriate Irene. He shrugged. 'Accidents happen.'

'They do,' Ivy said. 'Everyone makes mistakes sometimes.'

She glanced down at him, her lips shaping into the tiniest hint of a smile.

'This isn't just a *mistake*, Ivy! Your *recklessness* has ramifications for the entire company. I don't think you do fully understand the gravity of the situation, and frankly I'm disappointed that you don't. I—'

'Mum,' Ivy said, cutting her off. 'I think you need time

to digest this news. I think we should go. I'll see you at the office, tomorrow.'

This was Angus's cue. He casually rose to his feet, then took his time saying goodbye to Ivy's sisters.

They didn't rush as they left the house. Ivy just walked with purpose, without saying a word, until they stepped out onto the terraced entrance to the Molyneux mansion.

The heavy door clicked shut behind them.

'Ivy—'

But then Ivy halted his words with her lips.

She kissed him as she hadn't kissed him before. It was more intense, more thorough—more *confident*.

She wrapped her hands behind his neck, tugging him as close as possible. Her body was plastered against his, chest to breast, hip to hip.

She kissed him, and he kissed her, until they were both breathing heavily, until Angus *needed* to drag her to the car, and then home, as quickly as possible.

But then Ivy took a step back, and ran her hands through her hair.

'Wow,' she said. 'I haven't pashed a boy on my mum's front doorstep before.'

Angus laughed. 'I always knew you were a rebel.'

CHAPTER TWELVE

IVY WASN'T SURE how she felt.

She wasn't sure how she was supposed to feel.

She hadn't expected to feel like this.

She felt...

Okay, mostly.

Not great. But okay. She'd spent so much time imagining what it would be like to tell her mother about her pregnancy that she hadn't really thought about what would happen *after*.

But she'd known it would be bad.

But it wasn't. It was...okay.

Ivy leant back against the headrest as Angus drove her home.

'I'm starving,' she said. 'I can order some takeaway when we get home if you like?'

The question sounded like something she'd say if she and Angus were the couple he'd implied they were, and inwardly Ivy cringed a little.

But although Angus slanted a look in her direction, he nodded.

'You're not going to faint on me before then?' he asked.

She smiled. 'No. I had a pretty good idea we wouldn't be eating dinner at my mum's, so I had a snack before we left.'

A fortifying most of a block of chocolate, actually.

But by the time Angus stopped the car at her place, the atmosphere between them had shifted.

At her mother's house, it had seemed almost like they

were a team—banded together against anything her mum could throw at them.

Afterwards, she hadn't thought twice when she'd flung herself into Angus's arms. It had just been the right thing to do, her way of releasing some of that tension. And, *wow*, it had felt good.

But really, her pregnancy announcement hadn't solved anything. She was over the first hurdle, but there were a whole crap load of hurdles still to come.

It had felt like a victory, but really it wasn't. Her bravado had been false.

Kind of like she and Angus were a team—but really, they weren't.

At the front door, in the pool of porch light, she paused as she fished for her keys in her bag.

'Why did you let my family think we were a couple?' she asked. She sounded more defensive than she'd intended.

'I figured it was one less thing you had to deal with tonight,' he said.

'Okay,' she said. 'But what happens now?'

'Nothing happens,' he said. 'One day you'll just tell them we've broken up.'

He made it sound so easy.

She'd found her keys, and stabbed at the lock, taking a couple of goes before the key slid in.

Then she shoved the door open, her movements stiff.

'Isn't that what you wanted?' Angus said, remaining on the porch while she stepped inside. 'Even right at the beginning? A fake boyfriend, to avoid the so-called scandal?'

Ivy wasn't sure why she was angry, but she definitely was.

'A fake boyfriend who kisses me sometimes,' she said. 'You kissed me, tonight.'

'I know,' she said, with a sigh. 'This is confusing.'

'Ivy, I can't offer you any more than—'

She held up her hands, her cheeks turning pink. '*No.* Stop. I don't want this either, so no need to let me down gently.'

No. She'd made this mistake before, with Toby—getting caught up in attraction and hormones. Letting her emotions lead her, rather than logic and common sense. A relationship with Angus was not a good idea. The way she lost control around him… No. She couldn't risk losing herself in some crazy idea about love, again.

But still…even if allowing anything serious—if allowing the hint of love—was not acceptable, maybe there was still an alternative?

'Maybe what I want,' Ivy began, searching for what she was trying to say, 'is a fake boyfriend, with benefits.'

A way to, once and for all, sate this *thing* between them. To get it over with. But with no false expectations. No risk.

There was a long, long pause.

'A fake girlfriend, with benefits,' Angus said, as if testing the concept out on his tongue. His grin was wicked. 'I think I can work with that.'

This time, Angus kissed her.

And Ivy kissed him right back.

For the first time in as long as she could remember, Ivy was late to work on Monday. She'd had no excuse—Angus had left before dawn for the barracks as he was back at work now that his wrist was fully healed. He'd woken her when he'd left, and kissed her gently on the forehead.

Not long after, her alarm had gone off.

But she hadn't been ready to get up yet, so she simply hadn't. She'd curled up beneath her doona and fallen asleep to the vague idea that she should probably reset her alarm—and fortunately the arrival of her driver at seven-thirty had later served as a sufficient alarm replacement.

In the end, she wasn't that late, not really. It wasn't even nine a.m., but even so her staff seemed not quite to know what to do with her.

Ivy didn't know quite what to do, either.

She wasn't as bothered by her lateness as she would've liked, which concerned her a little.

But then, today she was doing all sorts of unfamiliar things—confronting her mother being number one on that list. So yes, maybe tardiness was the least of her worries.

Later that morning, Ivy took the lift to her mother's office.

It was on the very top floor, a floor above Ivy's offices, and was a hive of activity. Ivy weaved her way past the network of open-plan workstations and glass-walled meeting rooms to reach Irene's suite, separated from the rest of the floor by heavy, jarrah doors.

But her mother's assistant looked confused by Ivy's appearance.

'I have a meeting booked with Irene,' Ivy said.

Theresa shook her head. 'No,' she said, 'Irene has cancelled all her meetings for the rest of the week. She's flown to a conference in Berlin.'

'Oh,' said Ivy. 'Of course!' She shook her head, as if she'd just made a silly mistake.

But this had never happened before.

Ivy would never have described her relationship with her mother as perfect.

For all they were the same, they were also very different—despite her mother's insistence that Ivy was just like her.

But in business, they *were* in sync. Together they'd run Molyneux Mining for nearly a decade, with Ivy's role growing year by year.

The conference in Berlin did exist, but they'd decided, together, that another senior executive could attend in their place.

Irene's sudden change of mind was not a business decision.

It was extremely personal.

For all her bravado last night in the face of her mother's
disappointment, it had been incredibly hard for Ivy.

But, she realised now, some part of her had hoped for
something different today. That after a night to sleep on
Ivy's revelation, Irene's reaction would be different.

After all, Irene had three children—*surely* she should
understand?

Surely some part of her would be excited to meet her
first grandchild? Just as April had said?

But no.

Ivy had, for the first time in her life, put her own needs
ahead of Molyneux Mining.

Her mother didn't like it. She would never like it.

And that hurt.

'You're counting again,' Angus said.

Ivy's gaze shot up to tangle with his, her lips now pressed
firmly together.

Then she sighed. 'I do that sometimes. Despite my best
efforts.'

They walked together from the car park to the front of
the nursing home.

'Nerves,' she continued. 'Stupid nerves. I used to do it
all the time, and I thought I'd grown out of it, but apparently
not.' A pause, then a pointed look. 'I blame you.'

'Me?' he asked, innocently. 'I don't make you nervous.
Hot and bothered, maybe?'

She glared at him.

'But you don't need to be nervous tonight. My mum
will love you.'

'And that's the problem,' she said. 'I always *know* I
shouldn't be nervous. That's the frustrating thing.'

They stood outside the glass door of Reception. Ivy rolled her shoulders a few times, and took a deep breath.

She was still dressed for work, in fitted trousers and a spotted silky blouse.

Angus leant close. 'You look gorgeous. You won't say the wrong thing. And if you do, don't worry—she probably won't remember anyway.'

Ivy's jaw dropped open. 'Isn't that in terribly bad taste?'

Angus grinned. 'Trust me, my mum would've been the first to make that joke. Come on, let's do this. I *promise* my mum won't bite.'

The nursing home was a small, boutique facility, made up of a collection of detached villas and a larger single-level building for the high-dependency patients, like his mum. Once through Reception, Angus led Ivy through the communal living and dining rooms to his mum's room. It was spacious, like a generous hotel room, with a bed, a small seating area, and a separate en-suite bathroom.

His mum sat on the couch, watching the ABC news.

'Angus!' she said, smiling at him as they entered the room.

This was a good start. On the very worst days—for both of them—Angus needed to remind her who he was.

'Mum,' he said, 'this is my friend, Ivy Molyneux. Ivy, this is my mum, Hillary.'

'Nice to meet you,' Ivy said. She held out her hand, which Hillary shook firmly.

Hillary glanced between the two of them. 'And?'

'We have some news,' Angus said. 'Can we grab a drink, first?'

Soon they were all settled with cups of tea, seated around the small coffee table.

Ivy was fidgeting. Subtly—by twisting her fingers in her lap—but fidgeting none the less. It made Angus smile.

Such a powerful, polished, woman.

Yet so…*Ivy.*

'So, Mum,' Angus said. 'Ivy and I are having a baby.'

Ivy's eyes widened, as did Hillary's.

Then his mum's eyes squeezed shut. The older woman twisted to face Ivy. 'I've forgotten you, haven't I?' she said. 'I'm so sorry. I do that a lot, now.'

'Oh, no!' Ivy said. 'You haven't met me before.' When Hillary raised an eyebrow, she added, 'I promise.'

Hillary's gaze zipped back to Angus. 'I feel I've missed something here.'

Angus smiled, and then—briefly, and significantly censored—told his mother how he and Ivy had met.

She smiled, and nodded, as he spoke.

Angus was relieved. He'd asked Ivy to come tonight because when he'd called the nursing home earlier, he'd been told his mum was having a good day. But that was never a guarantee.

And it was important to him that Ivy met his mum. Stupid really, but somehow, given he was beside her when she told her family, he felt it should be the same with his.

His mum would never be as she had been—the woman who would've put Ivy instantly at ease and talked her ear off about all manner of random things.

But at least tonight she was a reasonable-strength version of his mum—not a version so diluted by dementia that he felt as if he was interacting with the disease, and not the mother he loved.

Now Hillary asked Ivy a bit about herself, but Ivy was talking too much, and over-explaining. Not Ivy's fault—he should've warned her—but he saw Hillary's eyes lose focus as all the words began to overwhelm her.

Ivy noticed too, and her sentence trickled out to nothing.

She looked stricken, and Angus reached out to squeeze her hand briefly. 'You're doing good,' he said, softly.

Then he asked his mum about her day. Hillary launched

into a detailed explanation, which might have been a true reflection of today, or an amalgamation of the last week or month—or have never happened at all—but regardless, his mum was animated again, her eyes full of life.

Ivy slowly began to relax back into her chair, her tea cradled in her hands.

'How is Scott?' Hillary asked Ivy, suddenly.

Ivy's body instantly stiffened, and her gaze flicked to Angus.

'Pardon me?'

'Scott is Carise and Tom's son,' Angus said. 'This is Ivy.'

But his mum shook her head firmly. 'No, no. I remember her. Long brown hair. Pretty blue eyes. Baby boy with a pink blanket because she believed in gender neutrality in colour schemes.'

This was the frustrating, awful bit. That a snippet of conversation from years ago could be remembered, but not the person his mother was talking to right now.

Ivy leant forward, placing her teacup carefully back in its saucer. 'My name's Ivy,' she said. 'I don't have a baby yet. But when I do, we'll bring him or her to visit you.'

Another agitated shake of the head. '*No,*' Hillary said. 'I haven't forgotten. I saw the wedding photos. Your husband is very, very handsome. Almost as handsome as my son.' She paused, looking thoughtful. 'But he got sick, didn't he?' Hillary balled up her fists, rubbing them into her eyes. 'Why can't I remember?'

'Mum,' Angus said gently, 'it doesn't matter.'

His mum turned back to Ivy. 'So, Carise, how is Scott?'

Ivy sent Angus another panicked glance. 'I'm not—'

'Scott is well,' Angus interrupted. 'He's walking now! Getting into everything. Tom is having to baby proof everything.' He forced a laugh. 'I guess I'll find out all about that soon enough.'

Hillary blinked. 'What do you mean?'

Hell.

It *still* hurt, every time.

'I'm going over to help Tom out with installing latches,' Angus said, improvising.

He had, actually. Three years ago, when Scott had started walking.

His mum seemed happy with that.

She also looked tired. Impossibly tired.

For the next few minutes he filled the silence, just as he always did. With bits and pieces about work, about things that happened years ago, things that happened today.

Hillary soon finished her tea, and Angus called a nurse to help her get ready for bed.

He kissed her on the cheek, and her hand reached up to curl into his hair and pull him close, just as she always had.

'I love you,' she said into his ear, as clearly and as firmly as ever.

A few minutes later, as they stepped outside the building, Ivy once again threw herself into his arms.

But this time it wasn't a kiss. There was nothing frantic or desperate in her action.

She simply hugged him. And held him.

'Who is Scott?' Ivy asked. 'And Carise and her husband?'

She'd propped herself up against her pillows, the sheet pulled up over her legs. She wore a faded navy singlet and her underwear, while Angus wore only boxers. Tonight was the first night they'd climbed into bed even partially dressed.

It was dark in Ivy's room, the only light glowing from a bedside lamp.

'Carise is the wife of an old friend, Tom,' Angus said. 'Scott is their eldest son, although they have a daughter now, too. Maybe more.'

It had been too long since he'd been in touch. Appallingly long.

'Were they close to your mum?'

Angus shook his head. 'No. They visited once to support me. I needed someone else who'd experienced my mum like that, you know? I had no family to come with me. To talk to about how I felt. I thought maybe if…' Another shake of his head. 'A stupid idea. It didn't help.'

'What happened to Tom?' she said gently. 'Your mum said he was sick?'

There was sympathy in her eyes, and Angus realised what that meant.

'He's not dead,' he said, very quickly. 'He wasn't that type of sick. I mean, he isn't that type of sick—cancer type of sick. He had PTSD.'

'Post-traumatic stress disorder.'

'Yeah. We worked together.'

Ivy nodded her head, as if that explained everything. 'Ah. That doesn't surprise me. You must deal with such awful, awful things.'

This bothered Angus.

'Why shouldn't it surprise you?' Angus said. 'It's what we train for. It's what we're *built* for. It's what we do. Why should it be such a shock that we manage to deal with it okay?'

His words were harsh, and far louder than he'd intended.

'I didn't say that,' she said. 'I just said I'm not surprised that some soldiers are impacted by PTSD.'

'And what does that make the rest of us? Robots?'

Ivy looked taken aback. She reached out for him, but he shifted a little so her hand fell to the sheet without touching him.

He knew he was being unfair. This wasn't about Ivy and what she'd said.

It was about his guilt. For a lot of things.

He slid from the bed, the thick rug beneath Ivy's bed soft under his bare feet. Despite how little he wore, Ivy's state-of-the-art climate-control system meant he wasn't at all cold.

Even that irritated him for some reason.

'It doesn't make you a robot,' Ivy said, very softly.

He had his back to her, but he could see her in the reflection of her ornate dresser mirror. She'd pushed herself up from the pillows, as if she'd been about to follow him, but had changed her mind.

'This is what you meant,' she said, after a while. 'At the gorge. You said that maybe it should be harder for you to go back. To go to war, to leave your loved ones behind. I didn't understand at the time.'

He shook his head. 'You wouldn't understand now.'

Why had he done this? He'd only needed to tell her enough to explain who his mum had been asking about. Ivy didn't need to hear any of this. He didn't need to answer any questions to do with this.

'No,' Ivy said. 'I'd never truly understand. But I can listen to you.'

Angus still watched her in the mirror. She hadn't moved. She looked beautiful, her hair loose, her face freshly scrubbed of make-up.

And she carried his child.

The scene was so domestic. They could be a married couple, thrilled at the impending birth of their first child.

Was this what had happened to Tom? Had he started to realise how much he had, and how much he had to lose?

Angus wanted to leave. He wanted out of this room and this domesticity.

But what would that achieve? If he went home, Ivy would still be pregnant. They were tied together for ever.

'When I go away,' Angus said, 'I won't be able to tell you where I'm going. Or what I'll be doing, or when I'll be back. Sometimes I'll get no warning at all, so neither will you. Sometimes I might be able to contact you when I'm away, sometimes I won't.'

Ivy's reflection nodded.

'I'll probably miss some special occasions,' he continued. 'Like birthdays. School assemblies, that type of thing.'

'How do you feel about that?' she asked.

'Not good,' he said. 'But not bad enough to quit my job.'

Ivy's eyes widened. 'It never occurred to me that you would.'

'Really?' he said. He turned to face her now. 'You think it's normal to still want to risk my life and to want to be away from home for indefinite periods of time now that I'm going to be a father?'

'I don't think what you do is normal,' Ivy said carefully. 'But that's why people like me do jobs like mine, and people like you are in the SAS. We're lucky there are incredibly brave, strong people like you. Australia is lucky.'

'How patriotic,' Angus said, his tone completely flat.

'Hey,' Ivy said. She pushed herself onto her knees, crawling to the edge of the bed so she was close to him. 'Don't dismiss what you do. What you do is important.'

'What a lucky kid we'll have,' Angus said. 'A mum who works seventy-hour weeks and a dad disappearing for months overseas.'

'I won't be like my mum,' Ivy said. 'I *won't*.'

'I know. You'll hire the very best nannies. And I'm hardly in a position to expect you to stay at home. I—'

She'd jumped to her feet, and laid her hand flat against his chest—although her push didn't move him an inch.

'Yes, I *will* hire a nanny, but not the way you think. I've already had preliminary designs drawn up for a nursery and play room on my floor at the Molyneux Tower. That way I can spend all my breaks, and lunch, with the baby. Plus I've been reading about breastfeeding, so this way I'll be able to continue after I return to work after six months.' She sighed, rubbing her forehead. 'I know it's not perfect. I've thought about maybe working part time, but I just can't, not right now. Maybe in a few years, once the company is more established under my leadership. So you're right, I won't win any mum of the year awards…but it's all I can do for now. I can't give up all I've worked for—' she snapped her fingers '—just like that.'

Her hand still rested on his chest, but it was gentle.

'I can't understand what you do,' Ivy said, 'but I *do* understand loving what you do. My sisters honestly believe I've been somehow forced into my role at Molyneux Mining, as if Mum managed to indoctrinate me into her mining executive regime, but it's not true. I love it. I love the challenge, the pressure, the responsibility. And maybe it makes me selfish not to give it all up, given I don't need to work at all. I could be a lady of leisure for every day of my life, and still have more money than I know what to do with.'

Now she took her hand away, so she could wring her fingers together.

'I don't think you're selfish for wanting to do what makes you happy,' Angus said.

'Ditto,' Ivy said.

But it wasn't the same.

'Tom used to be like me,' Angus said, unsure why he was trying to explain. 'We even look kind of the same, about the same height, weight, brown hair—that kind of thing. We did the selection course together and then the eighteen-month reinforcement cycle. We were even assigned to the same squadron and deployed together. Tom was great. I thought I was an insane trainer, but Tom sometimes out-did me. We pushed each other, we competed against each other—we were both just so proud to have made it. We loved the training—honestly, when you get paid to jump out of a helicopter, to storm a passenger ferry or to abseil down a skyscraper, you can't really believe it. We couldn't wait for our first mission.'

He paused, rubbing absently at his bare belly.

'He was fine, at first. Or I thought he was. He asked me, once, whether I ever had bad dreams about what we'd done, and seen, but I hadn't. I lied though, told him I had. Then he got married, had Scott. Maybe that made it worse? I don't know. He started seeing one of the psychs at work. He never told me—he never told any of us. But I started hearing rumours, you know?'

'Did you talk to him about it?'

Angus shook his head. 'No. I didn't really want to know. To believe it.' Which made him a pretty rubbish friend. 'Shortly after, he was seconded to a non-combat role. And we gradually drifted apart.'

'Why?'

'I don't know,' he said.

But that wasn't true. He just hadn't let himself think about it. So he tried again.

'I think,' he said, 'that it made me look at what I do, at what soldiers do, differently. It made me start to think that if someone as strong, as brave and as elite as Tom could be affected in that way, that maybe it might happen to me. At first, it was almost like I thought it could be contagious or something.'

He laughed without humour.

'But really, it wasn't that. I wasn't worried about it happening to me, because I know it wouldn't. It's been years now. I've been on many more missions. I've seen a hell of a lot. And I'm exactly the same. *Exactly.* I come back home, I debrief, and I carry on with my life. There's this other guy at work, now, who has just been diagnosed with PTSD. There has been at least one other I know of, too. I've read a bit about it. About guys who can't switch it off when they come home. Who patrol their home, who drive all night, who jump at every little unexpected sound. Yet I'm completely, completely fine.'

'So you think there's something wrong with you.'

'No,' he said. 'I know there are crazies in the army. People who get a kick out of death and destruction. But that's not me. For me it's a job. It's about doing what I've been trained to do: protecting my mates and achieving the mission.'

Ivy touched him again, and he realised he'd turned from her, and was staring at the bedspread.

Her fingers brushed his arm, then fell away.

'You think there is something wrong with you because you're not Tom. Because you are capable of doing your job, and also living your life.'

He rubbed at his eyes. He knew she was right; he'd had the same thoughts himself, many times.

But to agree, to voice it…

'I'm lacking something,' he said. 'I shouldn't be able to leave so easily—to walk away from my mum, my girl-friends and now from my child, and risk everything…for what? At the end of the day it's a job. A pay packet, no matter how anyone wraps it up in patriotic propaganda.'

'I think you're wrong,' Ivy said.

He faced her. She was wrong.

She'd asked why he didn't have a girlfriend at Karijini. He knew why—he didn't want a wife, a family that he'd leave again and again without issue. It wasn't fair to them.

It couldn't be normal to be like he was, to be so intrinsi-cally a soldier that nothing seemed to impact him.

Maybe he was a robot. A machine.

Ivy was looking at him with so much emotion in her eyes. She wanted to help him, he knew. But he couldn't be helped.

This was who he was.

And right now, he didn't want any help. He didn't want

words, or reassurances, or all those things that he supposed a wife or partner would offer.

But he still wanted Ivy.

So he reached for her, pulling her roughly against him.

Her eyes widened, but then her hands crept up to his shoulders.

He kissed her, and he wanted it to *just* be a kiss. A physical thing, a carnal thing.

So he wasn't gentle with her.

He held her hard against him, but she just gripped him harder back, kissing him with lips and teeth and tongue.

His hands gripped her bottom, and she wrapped her legs around his waist, rubbing herself against him.

'Angus,' she breathed against his lips.

But he didn't want that, he didn't want any more talking, any more words.

He turned, practically tossing her on the bed, then following her immediately, covering her with his body.

He kept half expecting her to push him away, to say this was too fast, too much...

But she didn't. Her hands were everywhere. Skimming the muscles of his chest. Her nails scraping far from gently down his back.

Somehow he got her singlet off over her head, and she helped him push down her underwear and throw it somewhere over his shoulders.

In between crazy, passionate kisses he tugged off his boxers. Immediately her fingers wrapped around his hardness, and he sucked in a breath, going still. Her mouth was at his shoulders, and she bit him gently.

He knew what that meant: *Don't stop.*

So he didn't. She was wet, hot, perfect.

And then he was inside her, and it was *more* perfect, more intense, more everything.

It was hard, it was fast, and all it took was Ivy moaning in his ear to push him over the edge.

He groaned, and he was gone.

For long minutes he lay collapsed partly on top of her, their heavy breathing gradually, gradually slowing.

But still, neither of them spoke.

For the second time tonight, Angus considered leaving.

But this time, because he couldn't see any point in staying.

And yet, when Ivy slid out of bed to go to the bathroom, he didn't move.

He saw the questions in her eyes when she returned. She'd expected a rapid escape as well.

But she didn't ask him to leave.

Instead, still without a word, she climbed back into bed. He reached for her, pulling her against him, her back to his chest.

And like that, they fell asleep.

CHAPTER THIRTEEN

'You're sure you want to do this?' Angus asked on Saturday morning.

'One hundred per cent,' Ivy said, her attention on her feet as she pushed down the clutch.

She sat in the driver's seat of her little silver hatchback. Not relaxed, of course, but surprisingly okay.

And *very* determined.

She wasn't going to let a mistake from her past have such an impact on her present, or her child's future, any more. She *needed* to do this.

'So I put the car into gear,' she said, moving the gear stick into first, 'then I turn on the ignition…'

This was the bit that had derailed her last time, and she tensed as she twisted the key.

But…*there*. The engine came to life. Not as loud and scary as she'd imagined.

But still. It wasn't exactly reassuring, either.

'Good job,' Angus said. 'Now—'

'I've got this,' Ivy interrupted. She had to do this herself. 'I release the handbrake, but my foot is still on the brake pedal, so I'm not going anywhere.'

Why did this have to be so complicated?

'And now I just need to gently press on the accelerator, while releasing the clutch…'

Hmm. This part was most definitely easier said than done.

'All I need to do is take my foot *off* the brake pedal, and put it *on* the accelerator, and the car will move forward.

And I have heaps of space ahead of me, so I needn't worry about flying into my front fence.'

Beside her, she knew Angus was smiling.

'So yes, start to release clutch, foot *off* the brake and *on*...'

The car moved.

At about two kilometres an hour, but it had most definitely moved.

'Oh, my God, I'm actually *driving*!'

'You're driving, Ivy!'

They were approaching her front gate at a snail's pace, but the road beyond it was still far too close.

'Turn left at the gate, Ivy. There's a school car park you can practise in only a short distance away.'

Very firmly Ivy pressed on the brake, and as she forgot all about the clutch the poor little Volkswagen jerked to an inelegant halt.

She patted the leather steering wheel in apology.

'Nope,' Ivy said. 'No roads today. How about you show me how to reverse back the way I've come, and we call it a day?'

'This will be the shortest driving lesson in history,' Angus commented.

'Or the longest, if you count the twelve years it took to get to this point.'

He nodded. 'Understood. Great job, Ivy.'

She grinned at him across the centre console. 'I know,' she said. 'Thank you.'

The next day, Angus drove her to that school car park.

It wasn't exactly vast, but the stretch of bitumen still gave Ivy a relatively reassuring margin of error.

He'd even brought along a couple of traffic cones, which he set up as a mock intersection.

Slowly—too slowly, according to Angus—Ivy practised starting, and stopping, and turning, and parking.

And after a lot of encouragement, going fast enough to make it into second gear.

That was met with raucous applause from the passenger seat.

When safely stopped, Ivy glared at him.

'You're not being particularly sensitive.' She sniffed. 'This is very difficult for me.'

Angus clearly knew she was being—maybe—just the slightest bit dramatic, and laughed rather dismissively.

'There isn't a lot of use in learning how to drive if you never go fast enough to actually *get* anywhere.'

Ivy glared at him. But this time, when they did a lap of the car park, she made it into third.

That afternoon, Ivy drove Angus, very cautiously, to the café where she'd met him for coffee. It felt as if it had been for ever ago, but it had only been a few weeks.

She was doing well. Really well.

A yellow square with a big black *L* on both the front and rear windscreen of the little Volkswagen proclaimed to all around them that Ivy was a learner driver. Although the way she crept along the street made that pretty clear, anyway.

He'd kept her on side streets, not wanting to frustrate other drivers, but now, at the café, there was only one parking space left, between two of the mammoth, European-badged SUVs that were standard for this area.

When Ivy realised this, she slowed so much that the car stalled, jolting them both forward in their seats.

'Dammit!' she said, smacking the steering wheel. 'I haven't stalled all day.' She glanced at Angus. 'Maybe you should park the car this time. That looks a bit tight.'

He raised an eyebrow. 'Ivy Molyneux is backing down from a challenge?'

Her gaze narrowed. 'Of course not. It's just…' A long pause. 'Of course not,' she repeated. And then restarted the car.

Just to increase the degree of difficulty, another car had driven up behind them. Unfortunately it was impossible for the driver to pass until Ivy had parked, with a concrete median strip keeping the other car immediately behind them.

Ivy had noticed, but she said nothing, her jaw clenched in concentration. The car rolled slowly forward, the indicator ticking loudly.

'Don't cut the corner,' Angus said. 'Remember to follow a wide arc, like we practised, so you are driving into the space straight.'

She nodded tightly.

She turned, but too abruptly. 'Too close,' Angus said, 'reverse a bit and try again.'

Second attempt was closer, but still not quite right.

With a sigh, Ivy reversed yet again.

The other driver was losing patience, and revved his engine.

Ivy was tense. Her gaze kept flicking to her rear-view mirror.

'Don't worry about him,' Angus said. 'You're doing fine.'

She bit down on her lip as she tried for a third time.

'That's it,' he said. 'Now straighten up.'

And that was it. She was parked.

The impatient driver sped off behind them, wheels squealing.

Ivy calmly clicked the handbrake into place, and turned off the ignition.

'I don't think that guy realised what he just witnessed,' she said.

'Or what a momentous occasion this is.'

'Exactly,' she said, with a wide smile. 'That was awesome. Let's go have a celebratory latte.'

Ivy practically bounced out of the car.

On the footpath, she turned to face him. 'I just *drove somewhere*, and *parked*,' she breathed.

She stood on her tiptoes, brushing her lips against his.

'I think that deserves a celebratory kiss, too,' she whispered.

Because he agreed—but that didn't meet Angus's definition of a kiss—he reached for Ivy again.

But he'd barely kissed her, when they were interrupted.

'*Eeeeeuuuuwwwwwwww!* Kissing!'

They broke apart. A small boy, maybe four, stood at their feet, pointing at Angus.

'That's gross.'

Angus grinned.

'Sorry, mate, but one day—'

'Scott!'

Both Angus and the boy turned at the deep male voice.

The man, the boy's father he assumed, was shadowed by the café awning. But he was tall, and familiar.

Angus froze.

Tom?

Then the man stepped out of the shadows, crossing the short distance to retrieve his son.

He had blond hair, like his son. It wasn't Tom.

'Sorry, guys,' he said. He nodded at Scott. 'He's got some pretty strong opinions at the moment.'

Then they were gone, continuing their walk down the street.

'Angus?' Ivy asked, curiosity in her eyes.

He gave a little shake of his head, needing to refocus.

'Do you know them?'

'No,' he said, his voice cracking slightly. He cleared his throat. 'Let's get that coffee.'

But something had shifted.

After coffee, Ivy drove them cautiously home, but for the first night that week he didn't stay.

When he walked in his front door, before it had even slammed shut behind him, he had his phone in his hand, scrolling down his list of contacts.

If Ivy could work past her fear of driving, he could do this.

But he still paused before dialling the familiar number. *For heaven's sake.*

He could go to war without even a single bad dream, and he couldn't make a damn phone call?

Angrily, he stabbed at the green dial icon, and pressed the phone too firmly against his ear.

It rang.

Almost immediately, it was answered.

'Angus?'

He needed to clear his throat.

'Tom,' he said. 'I'm sorry.'

Irene Molyneux was back.

Ivy stood alone in the elevator as she travelled from the ground floor of the tower direct to her mum's offices. No mucking around today—her first order of business was to talk to her mother.

The elevator walls were mirrored, and she stared at her own reflection.

Did she look different?

She knew about the whole pregnancy glow thing, but did it happen this early?

She was seven weeks now. Seven weeks and…two days?

Her tummy looked the same, anyway. Although that would change soon, if her appetite carried on as it had been.

She smiled. On Saturday night, she'd eaten almost an entire pizza.

Angus had seemed rather impressed. Ivy had been mildly horrified.

It had been fun, though, sitting cross-legged in front of some random Saturday night movie, eating pizza out of cardboard boxes, and garlic bread from amongst infinite layers of aluminium foil.

Ivy didn't remember ever feeling so relaxed with her other boyfriends. Angus made her laugh so easily, and he was quick to laugh himself. He…

He's not my boyfriend.

She dug her nails into the palms of her hands.

And, after last night's abrupt disappearance after she'd driven them home from the café, that *he's not my boyfriend* reality had only been underlined.

The elevator dinged as it came to a stop.

This wasn't the time to be worrying about glowing, or pizza, or non-boyfriends, anyway.

The doors slid open, revealing the organised chaos of Irene's floor.

Ivy wore her favourite suit today. A charcoal-grey pencil skirt and a short fitted matching jacket.

Her hair was up, looped into a neat bun, and she wore the pearl stud earrings her mother had given her the day she started work at the family business.

She wore them to work every day, but today—as she'd pressed the backs of the earrings into place—they had felt significant.

Silly, really.

She hadn't booked a meeting, but when her mother's assistant immediately ushered into her office it was clear Irene had been expecting her.

Of course she had.

In so many ways, they were *so* similar.

'Ivy.'

Her mum pushed back her high-backed leather chair, stood and stepped around her desk.

Good. She hadn't wanted to talk across that wide expanse of marri.

Because this *wasn't* business. Whatever her mother might think.

'Mum,' she began, ignoring her mother's gesture to take a seat. This wouldn't take long. 'I'm not going to apologise for being pregnant. I'm sincerely sorry for the inconvenience this will cause the company, but I'm not sorry I've decided to proceed with this pregnancy.'

Irene remained silent.

'All senior executive appointments at Molyneux Mining offer three months' full maternity pay, with the opportunity to take up to nine months' subsequent unpaid leave with your position held for you. I see no reason why this would not apply to me.'

Still complete, unreadable silence.

Her mother's gaze was steady, revealing nothing.

'Given the unfortunate timing,' Ivy continued, 'I'd like to take only six months' total leave. I know you only took six weeks with each of us, but I just don't think I can do that—'

Irene's gaze had dropped, and Ivy realised she'd laid her hands on her stomach.

Despite everything, Ivy's mouth curved into a smile.

She always smiled, now, when she thought of her baby.

She met her mum's gaze, trying to remember where she'd got to in her well-practised speech. But she couldn't find those words, when she realised her mother was smiling, too.

'I think that's a good idea,' Irene said. 'Six weeks wasn't long enough with any of you.'

Ivy blinked. 'Pardon me?'

'I'm comfortable maintaining my position throughout the period of your leave,' Irene said. 'Although I assume you will be returning full-time after that?'

The pointed question was almost reassuring—Irene was still very much her mother, not some strange transplanted alien.

Ivy nodded. 'Yes.'

A sharp nod. 'Good. I have heard about your plans for a nursery downstairs.' She sniffed. 'Such options weren't considered thirty years ago. I'm sure you'll find it incredibly distracting.'

Ivy opened her mouth—but was stopped with a glare.

'Although I'm sure if anyone can juggle such an arrangement, you can.'

Ivy was so stunned, that she simply mutely nodded.

'It occurred to me,' Irene said, 'on the flight home from Europe, that things have changed considerably in the past three decades. A woman in my role was unusual back then. I couldn't afford to be the mother I wanted to be, *and* the businesswoman I knew I could be.' She shrugged. 'Life is all about choices.'

And for the first time, ever, Ivy wondered if her mother questioned hers.

'Thank you,' Ivy said, because it seemed like the only appropriate thing to say.

'However,' Irene said, marching back behind her desk. She slid open a drawer on silent runners, and emerged with a thick white envelope. 'The circumstances of your pregnancy are less than ideal.'

She remained on the far side of the desk. The softness that had intermittently lightened her gaze had gone.

Right now, Irene Molyneux was all business.

'I've had our lawyers draft a contract for your...' she waved her hands in a dismissive gesture '...*boyfriend.*'

'He's not my boyfriend,' Ivy said. She wasn't interested in pretending any more.

But Irene barely blinked.

'Regardless, you're not married, or known by the public or our shareholders to be in a long-term relationship. When announced, particularly given the timing, it will be clear that this pregnancy is unplanned. Which is not what the public expects of *Ivy Molyneux.*'

Her mum made her name sound like a brand.

'However I feel it is somewhat realistic that you would keep a long-term relationship secretive. Hence I'd like our story to be that—'

'No,' Ivy said, as firmly as she'd ever said the word.

'Pardon me?' Irene said, her eyes narrowing.

'There will be no contract,' Ivy said. 'I'm embarrassed to say that I had exactly the same plan, myself.' She laughed dryly.

'Mr Barlow wouldn't sign?'

'He never will, no matter what we offer him,' Ivy said, 'but that's not the point.'

'Don't be ridiculous,' Irene said. 'Everyone has a price.'

Ivy actually snorted. 'Angus doesn't.'

Using his first name was a mistake.

Irene's expression became probing.

'You love him,' she said, dismissively.

'I *don't,*' Ivy said, but not quite immediately.

Love wasn't something you were allowed to consider when your relationship was based around sex and an accidental pregnancy, was it?

She squeezed her eyes shut for a long second.

'This isn't about Angus,' she said, deliberately saying his name again. 'This is about *me.* I'm not prepared to lie about this, to anyone.' She shrugged. 'I thought like you, a few weeks ago. A few days ago, even. That this was a disaster. That this could ruin my reputation. People would lose faith in me. Our stock price would crash. Our new magnesium deal would be in jeopardy. The world would end.'

It sounded ridiculous now. Yet she'd been so earnest when she'd said it all to Angus.

'I'm allowed to make a mistake, Mum,' she said. '*We're* allowed to make mistakes. Even someone like you, who never, ever does. It's not healthy to cover everything up. To pretend we're always perfect.'

'Mila said you're learning to drive,' Irene said abruptly.

'Yes,' Ivy said.

'I suppose you think I was wrong to do that.'

She meant what she'd done that night Toby had died. She didn't need to elaborate.

'I was protecting you,' Irene said. 'I knew what you were capable of. I couldn't let you destroy your future.'

'But I don't think I would've,' Ivy said. 'That night changed my life. But I never got to process it like a normal person. To deal with it. I should've learnt that I needed to trust my instincts, to be strong, to do what I knew was right. But do you know what I learnt instead? That it's not okay to make mistakes. *Ever.*'

'I've never said that,' Irene said. 'I would never tell you that.'

Ivy shook her head sadly. 'You didn't have to.'

She walked towards her mother. The room was absolutely silent now, and her heels echoed loudly on the polished wooden floor.

She reached for the large white envelope, tugging it from Irene's hands. Then turned, and dropped it into the recycling bin beside the desk.

'Mum,' she said. 'I love you. Thank you for delaying the handover of Molyneux Mining to me, and for understanding my need to take maternity leave. I love Molyneux Mining, and I'm incredibly proud that you have entrusted me with it. But I need you to also trust that it's okay that

I made a mistake and I can't fix it, or control it. That it's okay I had a one-night stand and ended up with a baby.'

At this, Irene sucked in a sharp breath.

Ivy smiled.

Irene didn't. But she did speak.

'I do trust you,' she said. 'I wouldn't be handing you the company, otherwise.' Then she reached out, grabbing Ivy's hand. 'But please be careful.' She met her gaze, and now it was her mum looking at her, not a powerful mining magnate. 'I don't know this Mr Barlow, or what type of man he is. But I do know it can be very, very difficult falling in love with the wrong man.'

'I'm not—' she began.

But Irene simply shook her head.

'I need to get back to work,' her mother said, all brisk and businesslike. 'So do you.'

'Of course,' Ivy replied.

And left.

CHAPTER FOURTEEN

THIS HAD BEEN a mistake.

Angus had an inkling as he opened his front door to let Ivy in.

And was absolutely sure by the time she stood in his kitchen and took in the two neat table settings at his dining table.

No, it was hardly white linen and candles—but it *was* a bit of an effort. Matching place mats. A jug of water. Cutlery in all the correct places.

It looked…romantic.

Which wasn't what he'd meant.

'Don't freak out,' he said, attempting to explain. 'This is supposed to be an apology for being a bit weird yesterday after we bumped into that guy and his son. Nothing more.'

Ivy's expression gave away little. 'Nothing more,' she repeated.

Great, so she understood.

Maybe.

He invited her to take a seat, anyway. She ignored the table, and slid onto one of the tall stools at the breakfast bar.

'Is that—' she asked, peering behind him and through the oven window '—*lasagne*?'

Angus shrugged. 'Possibly a bad joke,' he said. The awkwardness back at the homestead that day hadn't been all that dissimilar to right now.

But Ivy smiled. 'I like bad jokes,' she said. 'Besides, I genuinely want to try your mum's famous lasagne.'

He grinned. As Ivy relaxed, so did the tense atmosphere.

Mostly.

As they talked about favourite meals Ivy still wasn't quite *right*. She was fidgeting, for one thing.

She'd put her hands on her lap to hide that familiar twisting and untangling of her fingers, but he knew she was doing it.

Her attention was also erratic. She seemed reluctant to meet his gaze, her own flittering off in random directions.

Yes. This was stupid.

Had she even cared that he'd rushed off last night?

Maybe she'd been relieved. They'd been spending so much time together.

More time than he could remember spending with any other woman.

That realisation made him a little uncomfortable, too.

'I called Tom last night,' he said, abruptly, keen to take his thoughts in a different direction.

'Really?' Ivy smiled. 'That's brilliant. Did you talk long?'

'No,' he said. Ivy's face fell. Angus smiled. 'But that's normal. I don't think I've ever had a long conversation on the phone with a mate. I rang him, I apologised for being a useless friend and asked if he'd like to catch up for a drink. He said yes.'

'That's good,' Ivy said. 'It was pretty obvious what happened yesterday. I'm glad you did something about it.'

He wasn't sure what would happen when he saw Tom, but at least he'd tried. If it was too little, too late, then he'd just have to deal with it.

'I should've said something last night,' he said. 'Rather than rushing off.'

Ivy nodded, but then stilled that subtle movement. 'Why?' she said. She wasn't looking at him; instead she appeared to be studying the bubbling lasagne. 'It wasn't any of my business.'

Angus walked to the fridge, grabbing the salad he'd made earlier.

He walked over to the dining table, plonking the bowl down between his two neat place settings.

He knew what Ivy was doing.

Hadn't he done this himself, many, many times?

When physical intimacy had begun to merge into even a hint of more?

It was just different with Ivy, of course.

Her pregnancy had added a complexity, a depth to their relationship that wouldn't have existed, otherwise.

Wouldn't it?

No.

'I told my sisters today that we weren't really a couple,' Ivy said, twisting on the stool to face him. 'I'm not much good at subterfuge, I've decided.' She paused. 'And I hated lying to them. I spoke to my mum, too. She's approved my six-month maternity leave.'

'That's good,' he said.

Their conversation was almost formal, now. It reminded Angus of that very first coffee, which Ivy had attempted to run like a business meeting.

It remained that way when they took their seats at the table and as Angus served the lasagne; their knives and forks scraping noisily against their plates.

Ivy discussed the obstetrician she'd selected, but didn't invite him to her first appointment in a few weeks' time. She'd keep him informed, of course.

Of course.

He was relieved. This *thing* had always had an end date.

He'd known, hadn't he, that tonight was a mistake? That he'd inadvertently set up a scene that could be misinterpreted? That Ivy might think meant more?

So it was good that Ivy had come to her own conclusion. That together they could end this amicably.

If part of him was disappointed, it was because he was still just as attracted to Ivy as he'd been when he'd seen her walk down that aisle in Bali. Even tonight, dressed in jeans, a T-shirt and an oversized cardigan, she was beautiful.

Of course he'd regret that he wouldn't get to touch her again. Kiss her again.

He'd thought he'd have longer.

But not too long. Too long would just confuse an already overcomplicated situation.

'Angus?'

He blinked. Clearly Ivy had been talking to him, but he had no idea what about.

But he smiled, and she repeated her question, and their formal, just slightly uncomfortable conversation continued.

At least the lasagne was delicious.

You love him.

Her mother's words still bounced about in her brain. It had been almost twelve hours since their meeting, and yet she still couldn't shake her mother's erroneous assumption.

Telling her sisters had helped.

It was good to lay it out so brutally: we met for the first time at April's wedding. We had sex. Now we're having a baby. The End.

April had been her usual starry-eyed self: *'Are you sure there's not something between you both? You seemed so natural together. So right.'*

But Ivy had laughed, and made absolutely no mention of their...affair? Fling? Thing?

It was irrelevant, anyway. Something short term based purely on physical attraction. No more substantial than what had happened on the beach in Nusa Dua.

Except for what you've told him. What he's shared with you.

Mila had been pragmatic. *'Maybe it's good you're not*

*in a relationship. At least that way you don't need to worry
about what happens when you break up.'*

Ivy stared at her dinner.

True to form, she'd made her way through a mammoth
slice of lasagne. Remnants of white sauce and a lone cham-
pignon were all that remained on her plate.

Conversation had spluttered out, although they'd both
made a good go at it.

But the atmosphere was just *wrong*. None of the ease
and the fun of before.

Which made sense, of course.

When she'd walked into Angus's kitchen and seen all the
effort he'd put in—and *then* the abject horror on his face
when he seemed to realise what all of that could imply…

Well, it had made a decision she'd already made just
that much easier.

This had to end. But now it would end, tonight.

She didn't want this, this faux intimacy, this illusion of
something more.

Angus *clearly* didn't.

She offered to help him tidy up, but she knew he'd refuse. It was best she left as soon as possible.

At the open door, Ivy's hand stilled before pushing open
the flyscreen.

She turned to face Angus.

He was close, very close. She needed to tilt her chin upwards to meet his gaze.

His front room was dark, and the light that spilled from
the kitchen threw Angus's face into shadows.

'It was fun while it lasted,' Ivy said, then cringed. 'Oh,
God, that sounded lame.'

Angus laughed, his teeth bright in the darkness.

Ivy rushed to make her exit, yanking hard on the flyscreen handle.

But Angus reached out, pressing his hand against the small of her back and turning her to face him.

How many times had he done that? Touched her there? Both firm and gentle?

He stepped even closer.

'This is probably not the done thing,' he said, 'but how do you feel about one last goodbye kiss?'

She should feel it was pointless. A stupid idea.

Instead, she stood on tiptoes, reaching for him.

His kiss was gentle. Without demand.

And still not familiar. Even now, when they'd kissed so many times, it was *still* exciting, *still* different. Still special.

Her fingers curled up into his close-cropped hair, pulling him closer, inviting him to deepen their kiss.

And he did, but she felt the shape of his smile the second before his tongue brushed against hers.

Oh, God.

He was so good at this. Maybe she was good at this too, because his hands were now firmer at her back, drawing her closer.

She smiled now as her body pressed against his. So strong, and tall, and broad.

The tone of the kiss was now far from gentle.

But it wasn't desperate, either. This might be their last kiss, but there was no need to rush.

Then he lifted her just off her feet, moving her to her left until her back was flat against the wall.

His hands slid around to sit at her waist.

His mouth broke from hers to trail along her jaw. His breath was hot against her ear.

'I know technically I said a goodbye kiss, but how would you feel about...?'

And Ivy giggled, and nodded her head, and pulled his mouth back to hers as his warm hands slid beneath her T-shirt.

There was no question this was unwise, and unnecessary—but then, couldn't the same be said for nearly everything that had happened between them?

And she just *couldn't* regret any of it. Any of it.

She knew she wouldn't regret tonight.

Soon Angus led her down the hall to his bedroom. He flicked on the light, and she was glad; she needed to see him.

She'd never been inside his house before tonight, but she barely glanced at anything but the bed.

She just wanted to get there as soon as possible. Wanted to feel Angus against her as soon as possible.

But then he was on top of her as she sank into the mattress, and that was all that mattered.

How he felt, how he made her feel.

So good.

Somehow their clothes were gone, and her fingers drew patterns on Angus's gorgeous bare skin.

She felt the need to remember this. To savour this.

Angus had slowed too. His hands traced her curves, sliding from thigh, to hip, to waist, to breast.

She'd thought before that every kiss they'd had was different.

But *this* was different again. *This* was almost reverent, as if the two of them were etching this moment in their memories.

As if it were special.

Angus kissed the hollow beneath her hip. Then her belly, working upwards.

She shivered, her hands now still on his shoulders. Enjoying this.

It wasn't *as if* this were special. *It was* special.

Or at least, it was special to her.

I love him.

Her hands gripped his shoulders as she finally admitted the truth to herself.

That truth was why she'd needed to end this tonight, why she'd decided she no longer had time for pretending and fake anything. Not because it was dangerous, and because she needed to protect herself—but because it was already too late.

She had a choice now. To push him away. To tell him this was a mistake and escape into the night.

That would've been the right choice. The smart choice. A last-gasp attempt at protecting herself. Protecting her heart.

He lifted his head, questions in his gaze.

But she didn't shove him away. Instead she slid her hands to his arms, as if she were capable of tugging him back up to her.

Although he still understood what she wanted, and slid his body upwards.

And he kissed her again. Again, and again, and it was exactly what Ivy wanted.

She wanted all of this; she wanted him here, close against her, inside her.

Afterwards, she knew she'd been right.

She wouldn't regret this. This last time together.

But she could certainly regret loving him.

Angus considered leaving a note.

Ivy was still asleep, curled on her side in his bed.

He was showered and dressed, and he'd packed yesterday before she'd arrived. He was flying out today—on a mission that he couldn't tell her about.

So yes, a note would be easier.

Instead, he sat on the bed beside her, and reached for her—shaking her shoulder gently.

It was still dark outside, and Ivy blinked as her eyes adjusted to the glow of his bedside lamp.

She stretched, reaching her hands above her head so they bumped against the headboard.

'Hey,' she said, all sleepy.

'Good morning,' he said. 'I'm off to work.'

'What time is it?'

'Early,' he said. 'Sleep some more. There's no rush to leave. I just wanted to let you know I'll be gone for a while.'

'How long?' she asked, suddenly appearing more awake.

His lips quirked. 'I can't tell you that. Or where I'm going.'

She nodded in understanding. 'Okay. But I'm not going to see you any time soon.'

He didn't quite know what to make of her expression, but he felt he needed to say something more.

'Last night was fun…' he began. Then realised what he'd said.

'Hey, that's my lame line,' she said. Then her gaze fell downwards. Her fingers tangled in the white bed sheet. 'But yes, it was fun.'

He went to stand, needing to go.

But she laid her hand on his thigh, and he went still.

'Angus—' she said. Then sighed. She lifted her gaze, meeting his head-on. 'Look,' she said, 'I know what we said. About this being the last time. I know what I said, about that stuff with Tom not being any of my business.' She paused, but her gaze didn't waver. 'But honestly, I did care. I did want to know. And last night I wanted to tell you all about what happened when I spoke to my mum yesterday. But I didn't, because I'd decided that this had to end.'

'Why?' he asked.

'Because if I didn't end it now, I was worried I'd never be able to end it.'

Angus remained silent.

'I know this isn't what we planned. I know this isn't what either of us wanted. And it's endlessly, impossibly complicated. We need to work together for another eighteen years at least, and we need to be civil. So ending it now *is* smarter. While we can walk away without hurt feelings and anger and disappointment.' For a moment, she looked down at her fingers, but only to pull them free of the fabric and lay them flat against her stomach. 'But what if I don't want to be smart? What if I'm not quite so scared of making mistakes any more?'

Not quite so scared.

But she *was* still scared. He knew what she was offering him. What she was revealing to him.

Her gaze was raw. Open. Emotional.

It was...

Overwhelming.

He didn't know what to think.

Last night he'd been so worried about her feelings that he'd made her dinner.

And that *had* been a mistake.

That was something he'd do for his partner. His wife.

That was why it had felt wrong. Because Ivy wasn't those things.

No one would ever be those things.

She was a woman who, through circumstance, he was having a baby with.

She was smart, and brilliant and beautiful—but that didn't matter.

He wasn't built for more than what they'd had.

He just wasn't wired that way.

Ivy had pulled back subtly, her body no longer leaning towards him.

'I can't,' he said, finally.

For a long while, there was silence.

'You're wrong,' Ivy said, eventually. 'You *can*. I know you think you're missing something. I know you think of yourself as some flawed, fighting machine.'

He wanted to argue, but he met her strong, determined gaze and knew he needed to let her speak.

Besides—hadn't he used the same words? To her, that one time, and to himself, many more?

'But, Angus,' she said, softly, 'you *do* care. You *do* feel. And you do those things so, so deeply.' She sighed, her lips curving into a sad smile. 'When I told you my plan, all those weeks ago, I'd been so sure you'd accept. I mean, who would pass up the chance to be an instant millionaire? But now I know exactly who can't be bought with money. The type of person who believes in honesty, and hard work, and doing things the right way, regardless of the cost.' She paused. 'A *good* man. A very good man. A man who wants to know the mother of his child, who insists on being a part of her life for the sake of his child—because he wants the very, very best for his son or daughter. A man who loves his mum, loves his friends, and—yes, I know you'll roll your eyes when I say this—loves the country he fights for.'

Her hand was still on his thigh, and she pressed her weight against him, as if to punctuate her point. 'You don't lack *anything*, Angus. You're capable of anything you want. Even love.'

It was only now Ivy's gaze wobbled, and then eventually drifted downwards.

He didn't know what to say. He hadn't expected this.

But then, he hadn't expected any of what he'd experienced with Ivy.

Her words continued to reverberate around his head, but they were too unfamiliar and too new for him to grab onto.

He'd taken far, far too long to say anything.

'I can't,' he said again. It was all he could say.

'Okay,' she said, and her hand fell away.

CHAPTER FIFTEEN

Five weeks later

APRIL WAS A *lot* more excited than Ivy was.

Her sister had grabbed a brochure from the ultrasound clinic's reception desk, and opened it up on Ivy's lap. They sat together in the waiting room, one other couple also waiting patiently in the corner.

'See,' she said. 'You can have your 3D scan etched into a *glass cube.'*

Ivy raised an eyebrow. 'How about we wait until we know that I have a healthy baby before we start ordering keepsakes?'

April bumped her shoulder against Ivy's. 'You'll be fine,' she said. 'I know it.'

It probably wasn't fair to think that April was more excited than Ivy was. Of course Ivy was excited. After all, today she'd get to *really* see her baby for the first time. It was just she was also nervous.

So nervous.

Silly, really. She'd visited her obstetrician only a few weeks earlier, and everything had been fine. Her baby's heartbeat was strong.

She'd tried to explain how she was feeling to her sisters, and they'd said the right things, but...

The thing was, it wasn't the same for them. It wasn't *their* baby.

Angus would understand.

Ivy tilted her head backwards until it bumped against the wall, staring up at the ceiling.

He'd emailed her a couple of times while he'd been gone, when he'd been at camp. She hadn't really expected that, although she supposed she should've. He'd never just disappeared, even when she'd wanted him to.

He'd been polite, asked how she was going, how the baby was. That was it—nothing else. Certainly no mention of their last conversation.

Despite everything, she hoped he'd be home soon.

Yes, a huge part of her cringed at what she'd said when she'd last seen him. When she'd so haphazardly laid her heart on the line.

It was *embarrassing.*

Mortifying. And a lot of other things.

But—she couldn't regret it.

She looked down at her tummy, at where the best mistake of her life was growing.

No. She had no regrets.

And so she did wish he were here. So he could tell her his latest titbit of baby development he'd gleaned from his research. So she could voice her concerns time and time again and not feel as if she were being a crazy person, because Angus would *get* it. He'd understand. He'd be all strong and reassuring and he would probably even hold her hand—just because she needed him to.

Of course even if that morning all those weeks ago had ended differently, he still wouldn't be here.

He'd warned her of the realities of his work, and she'd understood—but it was still hard.

She didn't have any right to miss him, not really. But their baby would.

She laid her hand on her stomach.

But she reckoned this baby would be pretty tough. This

would be their reality—Daddy away for weeks or months at a time. But back for long stretches, also.

And this baby would be *loved*. So loved. Angus would love this baby with all he had. He already did, Ivy was sure.

And wasn't that what mattered, really? Love?

The sonographer walked into the reception room, and called out Ivy's name.

April grinned, immediately jumping to her feet, and Ivy followed behind her.

Minutes later she lay on her back, her still-pretty-flat tummy exposed and smeared in gel.

The sonographer explained what she was doing, and directed Ivy's gaze to a screen mounted above her and to the right. 'You'll be able to see everything there.'

And then she could see everything.

A baby. An actual tiny baby with arms and legs and a fluttering, healthy heart.

Tears stung her eyes and crept their way down her cheeks.

April gripped her hand, and smiled, with tears making her own eyes glisten.

Ivy loved this baby with absolutely everything she had. With an intensity she hadn't thought possible.

Her whole life had been about her career. Every day she'd woken up to thoughts about work and gone to sleep after checking her email. Her weekends had simply interrupted her business hours—and, while she'd had some vague, future plan of maybe, maybe one day getting married, it was always to the most sensible, the most appropriate of men. Certainly not men that made her skin tingle or who took her breath away.

She used to think she was being wise in her dating choices. That she'd learnt from the mistakes of her past, and was ensuring that she'd never again fall in love as recklessly as she had with Toby. She'd believed she needed to protect herself from the loss of control that love seemed inevitably to bring.

But now, now that all these years later she'd fallen in love again, she knew how wrong she'd been.

She hadn't put up barriers to protect her career, or to re-tain control—not really. She'd put up barriers because Toby had been her first love—and, however misguided, losing him had *hurt*.

She hadn't wanted to feel that way again.

But despite her best efforts, here she was.

Desperately in love with a man who didn't love her.

And it hurt. So much.

She knew what she'd told Angus had been right—that he was capable of loving her.

The problem was, he didn't.

But this baby in front of her, wide awake and rolling unhelpfully for the smiling sonographer, he or she *would* love her.

And, for now, that would be enough.

The Friday he arrived home, after just over five weeks away, Angus visited Tom.

The days were getting longer now, and Tom and Angus sat on the edge of Tom's timber decking as Tom's two kids ran about the backyard in the fading sunlight.

Carise had hugged him, hard, when he'd arrived, but said barely a word.

She was clearly glad he was here, which surprised him.

Being invited here had surprised him, too.

Surely deserting your friend in his time of need nixed any future dinner invitations? It would seem not.

Although Tom was, understandably, cautious, and far from the jovial, loud man that Angus remembered. Was that the PTSD? Maybe. But Angus guessed that, tonight, it was mostly his fault.

Tom didn't know what to expect of his supposed mate who'd just so randomly dropped back into his world.

Angus didn't blame him.

For a while, they both quietly sipped their beers as they watched the kids.

'Scott is getting tall,' Angus said, just to say something.

'Yeah. Amber will be tall, too, I reckon,' Tom replied.

Then that was that.

'Mate,' Angus said, trying again. 'I'm so sorry for—'

'Yeah,' Tom said, cutting him off. 'That was pretty low.'

'I'm sorry,' he repeated, because—if nothing else—he could at least just keep saying that again and again.

His friend sighed. 'I know,' he said. 'I know it wasn't like I told you what was going on, not really, but I'd kind of hoped you'd ask. You know?'

Angus nodded. Yes, he knew.

'I was—' he began, but that wasn't right. 'I thought—' But that wasn't right either. 'I didn't understand,' he went with, eventually. 'I didn't understand at all.'

Tom smiled, squinting a little now that the sun was low, peeking between the trees along his back fence.

'You still don't understand,' he said.

'No,' he agreed. 'I'm sorry, I don't.'

Tom slanted him a pointed look. 'Stop apologising or I'll have to ask you to leave.'

And that comment was *so* much like the Tom that Angus remembered that Angus grinned, holding his glass and spare hand up in mock defence. 'Okay, you get that I'm sorry.'

Tom nodded.

'It was hard for me to tell you,' Tom said. 'Especially you. We'd been along this SAS journey together, and I'd just seriously derailed. You were still strong, and I was weak. A failure.'

'No, Tom—'

Now his friend held up his hand. 'Nah, I know. I'm not a failure for having a mental-health issue—and I have a se-

riously brilliant therapist who has helped me realise that.'
He paused. 'She's helped me with a lot of things, actually.
Reprogramming my thoughts and reactions in certain situations, that type of thing. I still have the occasional bad
dream, but mostly I'm all good.'

Angus smiled. 'I can see that.' And he could. There was
an ease to Tom that was new, and a calmness. 'But do you
ever miss it?'

The challenge of what they did. The adrenalin rush.

Tom smiled. 'I knew you'd ask. But the answer is simple:
no. I have a new career now. I've just got my builder's ticket,
and my business is going well. I choose my own hours, I get
to spend more time with my kids…it's great.' He downed
the last of his beer. 'But then, it was always different for you,
wasn't it? The regiment is more than a career for you. It's your
life. It's who you are.'

It's who you are.

But was it?

He thought of the past five weeks, and the complex international training exercise with a close Australian ally
he'd just completed. It had been tough, it had been chal-
lenging, and he'd learnt a hell of a lot.

And he'd loved it. Loved every last second of it.

So yes, the SAS was who he was. Since his father's death
it had been all that he'd wanted, and now he'd made it, it
was all he ever wanted to do.

But for the first time maybe he needed to ask a different
question. Was the regiment *all* he was? Was it *all* he wanted?

A familiar musical jingle jolted Ivy out of her lovely deep
sleep.

She blinked, staring up at her ceiling. Light streamed
in through her lounge-room window—but then, that was
to be expected in the middle of an almost summer Sunday afternoon.

Ivy swung her legs off her couch, and padded on bare feet down the hall to the intercom panel near her front door.

'Hello?'

'It's Angus.' His voice was just as delicious as she remembered. 'Are you okay?'

'Of course,' she said, surprised. 'Why wouldn't I be?'

'You didn't answer your phone,' he said. 'Can I come in for a bit?'

She pushed the button that would let him in, then unlocked and opened her front door, before heading into the kitchen.

She grabbed the CD she'd had copied for Angus at the ultrasound clinic, and checked her phone. Three missed calls from Angus while her phone had been on silent during her nap.

For some reason that made her smile.

Angus's heavy footsteps approached down the hallway.

When he stepped into the room, he seemed bigger than she'd remembered. Even taller.

He was dressed casually, a white T-shirt, dark shorts and flip-flops. It had become warm while he'd been gone, and today it really did feel like summer. Especially for Ivy, given her body's thermostat seemed permanently set about five degrees hotter than before she was pregnant.

As always, the weight of Angus's attention did all sorts of things to Ivy's tummy. She'd need to work on that reaction; it was hardly helpful.

She was dressed in the girly version of his outfit—white shorts, red singlet, no shoes. She hadn't expected any visitors today, and she knew she was all creased from her nap, but Angus *still* made her feel as if she were the most stunning woman he'd ever seen.

Maybe that was just how he looked at all women? Regardless, it wasn't helpful, either.

'Any bump yet?' he asked.

He crossed the room, but he seemed...different. He always seemed so relaxed, so confident, so comfortable—but not today.

She shook her head. 'Not yet. A few extra kilos, but I can't blame the bub for that.' Ivy held out the CD. 'Here, so your visit to make sure I'm still breathing isn't wasted. I'm not sure if you saw that photo I emailed you, but here are the rest. Personally, I think the 3D images are a little creepy.'

'Thanks,' he said. He rotated the CD case in his hands a few times. 'I didn't just come to check on you. I called because I wanted to talk to you.'

'Okay,' Ivy said. She gestured vaguely at the couch, and then her bar stools. 'Take a seat?'

He shook his head. 'No, I—' He flipped the CD case a few more times. 'Ivy,' he said. 'I want to talk to you about my dad.'

That was about the last thing she'd expected him to say, but she simply nodded.

'I told you that my dad died when I was seventeen,' Angus said. 'But I didn't tell you what happened.'

'You said it was sudden,' Ivy said, remembering.

'Yeah. Although it wasn't an accident, or an illness—he stepped in front of a train the day he realised he'd lost the family business.'

'Oh, Angus—' Ivy began, instinctively stepping towards him.

But he shook his head. 'I used to be so proud of him. He started with only one furniture shop, and ended up with thirty. He took us from a ramshackle house to a mansion. But that was the problem, in the end—he overexpanded. Took one too many risks.' Angus shrugged. 'That's what I don't get though. I *know* he could've started again. He'd had nothing before, and Mum and I didn't care about the flash house, school and car. I'm still angry at him about that.' He paused for a long time.

He took a step towards her now, but then seemed to change his mind, and remained where he was. 'Anyway—

the point of all this, and I promise there is one, is that when my dad died, I couldn't sleep.'

'That makes sense,' Ivy said, but she was completely confused.

Angus's lips curved upwards without humour. 'I'm not very good at this. Maybe we should sit down.'

He led her to her couch, and they sat, side by side—but with a good-sized polite gap between them.

'I've always been a great sleeper,' Angus said. 'But when dad died, I just couldn't. Which I'm sure is normal. It went on for months—months of tossing and turning and snatches of sleep, and it certainly didn't get any better as Mum started to get sick. Then one night, I slept, and I was back to normal. And that only happened once I'd finished school and joined the army. It was like my subconscious could finally rest again amongst the rigidity and structure the armed forces gave me.'

He leant forward, putting the CD on her coffee table with a clatter. He remained leaning forward, his elbows resting on his knees as he looked at Ivy.

'The night you told me you were pregnant, I couldn't sleep,' he said. 'That was the first time since Dad died that's happened. But then, once I got my head around the idea and even feeling good about it—everything went back to normal.'

He sat up properly now, turning slightly so he faced her.

'Until two days ago. I had an awful night's sleep on Friday. And an even worse one last night.'

Ivy had no idea where this was going. 'I'm sorry?'

His smile was subtle. 'You should be, given it's your fault.'

'I'm lost,' she said. She'd never seen Angus like this. There was an uncertainty in his gaze she was completely unfamiliar with.

'I used to think there was something wrong with me because I didn't have Tom's nightmares, or that I was some robot because I enjoy the challenge of combat. I thought because I could walk away so easily from my girlfriends to go to war, because I never missed them—and because I was never that excited to see them when I returned—that I had to be lacking something. As if when my dad died and my mum got sick that my ability to love had gone with them. I thought that all I was was my job, and that, yes—maybe I was just a fighting machine incapable of emotion.'

Had he shifted on the couch? Or maybe she had, because now their knees were almost touching.

'But I worked out that I'm not sleeping because my life has been knocked off kilter, and until I set it right again it's not going to get any better. And the reason I'm floundering so badly—both right now and when I try to get some sleep— is because of you, Ivy. Meeting you has changed everything.'

'So you want me back in your life so you can get some sleep?' she asked, only half joking.

'No, I want you back in my life because I love you.'

And Ivy was so stunned she said absolutely nothing at all.

'I've realised I was wrong. It isn't that I'm not capable of emotion, or of falling in love—I just wasn't prepared to take that risk. And before you, I certainly hadn't met someone where that risk even seemed an option. I know how devastating it is to lose the people you love, and for the past fifteen or so years it's been a hell of a lot easier just to distance myself from all of that. If I don't love someone, it's easy when I'm deployed. It's easy to walk away.' He caught her gaze. 'You were right the other night, you know, but I wasn't ready to hear it. I had too many years of believing what I'd been telling myself, that I couldn't comprehend anything different.'

They'd both moved closer now, their knees bumping together.

'I used to think...*love* was dangerous,' Ivy said. The word was still hard to say, even if the echoes of Angus's declaration still rang in her ears. 'I thought love would cause me to lose control. To make poor decisions. To lose myself.' Her lips quirked. 'And, well—I was right about the control bit. I'm not quite myself when I'm with you, and that scared me. But the thing is, I've realised I'm *not* nineteen any more. I'm an adult, and my own person, and I'm not about to get swept up in silly delusions and daydreams. And yes—maybe it doesn't hurt if I lose control, now and again. You've even helped me learn that it's okay if I make mistakes.'

Angus reached out to still the hands that she barely realised she was twisting and untwisting together. He held them between his, his touch warm and reassuring—but, even now, shooting shivers along her skin.

'You're amazing, Ivy Molyneux,' he said. 'Amazing, and strong, and smart, and beautiful. I made the worst mistake of my life that morning, but I hope like hell I'm not too late to fix it now.'

Ivy looked down at their hands. At first she'd kept her hands still, but slowly she shifted her fingers, until their hands were linked together.

She leant closer, then lifted her gaze until it tangled with his.

'I love you,' she whispered against his mouth. 'You and our baby weren't part of any of my plans, but you've turned everything upside down in the most wonderful, perfect way. I guess that's how love is supposed to work? Without any plans.'

'Yeah,' Angus agreed, his breath warm against her skin. 'No plans. But lots of risks and probably more mistakes along the way. Are you okay with that?'

Ivy nodded as she smiled. 'Oh, yes,' she said.

She closed the infinitesimal gap between their mouths with a soft kiss.

'We all make mistakes, Angus,' she said, 'but I know I'm not making one now.'

EPILOGUE

It was a beautiful day for a wedding.

Once again, an aisle stretched before Ivy. Once again, guests twisted on their white wooden chairs to look in her direction.

But today, it wasn't beach sand that she walked upon.

Instead, her path was a dusty red, her destination the dappled shade of a boab tree.

It was late October in the Pilbara, the sun warm—but not harsh—against her skin. Ivy walked to the gentle sounds of an acoustic guitar duo, the only sound amongst the surrounding silent landscape of Bullah Bullah Downs.

Until Nate began to cry.

Instantly, every guest's attention shifted to the pram that Irene Molyneux pushed back and forth, just to the left of the rest of the bridal party. Ivy's sisters, in their emerald-green dresses, abandoned their posts beside the swollen trunk of the Boab to coo somewhat helpfully—but it was Angus, in tailored shorts and an untucked white shirt, that immediately took action.

By the time Ivy stood beside him, her son was cradled against Angus's shoulder, and his cries had quietened to a half-hearted whine before spluttering out to a contented sigh. Angus smiled at Ivy, then kissed Nate's dark head.

Irene gestured to take Nate back, but Ivy shook her head.

Nate was happiest in his dad's arms, anyway.

A moment later Mila, April and Tom were all back in place, and Ivy, Angus and Nate stood before the celebrant.

A year ago, in Nusa Dua, Ivy never would've imagined any of this. A son, a soon-to-be-husband, a wedding.

Her whole life had been her career, her entire focus on Molyneux Mining.

But now—everything had changed.

Her career was still important, but it could wait a few more months.

Since Nate's birth, life had been a blur—but a different type of blur from before. Rather than meetings and emails and negotiations it was all about feeding, and nappies and—if she was lucky—sleep.

She couldn't say she loved every aspect of motherhood so far—especially not those three a.m. feeds—but she definitely, definitely loved Nate.

'You okay?' Angus asked, softly, as the celebrant introduced herself to the guests.

He was so handsome in the dappled light. His hazel eyes were gorgeous, and even now they made her heart leap whenever he looked in her direction. And he was a wonderful father. He'd been home for Nate's birth, and then gone for eight weeks. It had been hard, for both of them, but now he was back for a few months and was making every moment with his son count.

Yes, she definitely, definitely loved Angus, too.

Ivy nodded.

'No step counting?'

Ivy shook her head, surprised at the question. 'No, not in months.'

Angus's gaze had knocked Ivy off her axis all those months ago, but her world had realigned now. Different, but better than she ever could've imagined.

'I did,' Angus whispered.

'Really?'

'I counted your steps,' he said, with a smile. 'As you walked down that aisle.'

'Why? Do I make you nervous?' she teased.

'No,' he said. 'I was counting backwards, counting down until you become my wife.'

'That's very romantic,' Ivy said, with a smile. Angus's gaze traced every line of her face, as if she were the most beautiful thing he'd ever seen. She'd never felt more loved. More happy.

He shrugged. 'Seemed the time for it.'

Ivy laughed. 'But—how did you know what number to start counting at?'

'Would you believe I had special SAS training?'

'I'd believe you got it totally wrong and ran out of numbers too early.'

Angus grinned as their son burrowed tighter against his shoulder. 'If I did, it was only because Nate distracted me.'

He leant closer, to whisper against her ear. 'I love you.'

'I love you too.'

Together, smiling, they finally turned towards the celebrant, and the ceremony began.

And as the words washed over Ivy she wasn't worried about counting her steps, or work, or what anyone thought—or expected—of Ivy Molyneux.

As she stood here beneath the Pilbara sun, surrounded by the people she loved, all that mattered was *this* moment, *this* man, and this amazing baby they'd made together.

She'd wasted so much time terrified she'd made the worst mistake of her life that night in Nusa Dua.

But instead she'd got everything—absolutely everything—spectacularly right.

* * * * *